The Billionaire's Christmas Baby

The Billionaire's Christmas Baby

Victoria James

Entangled Publishing, LLC
2614 South Timberline Road
Suite 109
Fort Collins, CO 80525
Visit our website at www.entangledpublishing.com.

Edited by Alethea Spiridon Hopson & Wendy Chen
Cover design by Tahra Seplowin

ISBN   978-1503056145

Manufactured in the United States of America

First Edition November 2012
Second Edition December 2013

To Andrew, my husband. You are my partner in life, my soul mate, my hero. All my love, always.

From the Author

Dear Reader,

I'm so excited to share this re-release of my very first Entangled Indulgence book with you!

The Billionaire's Christmas Baby is very near and dear to my heart. I adore the holidays, so much so that on November 1st, I begin decorating our house for Christmas. The holidays have always been a special time and growing up I was very blessed to be surrounded by a large, extended family. Gatherings were loud and exciting, and filled with love and delicious food. It was after I had my own children that I began reflecting on who I am as a person, and how much of that is based on how I grew up. What if I'd had no one? Or if I'd had everything and then had it all ripped away from me? I would be a very different person than I am today. Those thoughts sparked my idea for Jackson and Hannah's story…

Jackson Pierce had it all at one time, only for tragedy to step in and shatter his childhood. He is now a man who wants nothing to do with Christmas and the memories that come with the season. He hates the holidays so much, that every year he escapes to his remote cabin deep in the woods. It takes a very special woman-and a very sweet baby-to make him want to open his heart to love again. Hannah Woods has always been alone and has had more than her share of pain, but she's always held onto her belief that good will triumph… and she's always believed in the magic of Christmas. Getting stranded during a blizzard with Jackson at his remote cabin is just the kind of opportunity Hannah needs to show him the real meaning behind the season…

I hope you fall in love with this couple as much as I have. And I hope that Hannah, Jackson, and baby Emily warm your heart and remind you of the magic of the season.

Happy reading and happy holidays!

Victoria

Prologue

Hannah hated Thursday nights.

All she felt like doing after counseling a group of single, unemployed mothers was changing into her penguin flannel pajamas, and having two glasses of wine and a large bag of fat and calorie-laden potato chips while watching mind-numbing television.

Luckily for her waistline she had nixed that habit after the first two months of the workshop when she spotted an emerging muffin top over her favorite jeans. Now she only allowed herself the indulgence once a month. And she had switched to half-the-fat organic chips. There was no point in killing herself one chip at a time just because she couldn't save the world and every child who ended up in foster care—or so she kept telling herself. Nights like this tested that theory.

Hannah jiggled the key until she heard the lock click shut on the ancient church door. She swung her bag over her shoulder and tread down the shallow stairs two at a time, her mind preoccupied by the woman who hadn't attended the meeting tonight, Louise. Her pace faltered on the last step and she paused despite the chilly wind. Something felt off. She slipped her BlackBerry out of her pocket and glanced down at the display. No messages. She bit her lower lip while she stared at the lit screen; she had expected a phone call from Louise. Maybe she'd stop by her apartment on her way home.

Hannah pulled her collar up, but instead of walking toward her car, she put her keys and BlackBerry back in her pocket and slowly turned to look at the church. The old stone structure stood like a comforting beacon, illuminated in the yellow glow of the old-fashioned street lamp. Snow fell like powdered sugar through a sifter and the faint scent of cedar was laced through the crisp late November wind. She knew this scene perfectly.

But something was different tonight.

A small cry rang out as clear as a singing bird at dawn. Hannah's eyes followed the sound. Her heart jerked when she spotted a Moses-like basket with pink lining sitting on the stone porch. Had she walked right by it? The massive oak doors towered over the tiny bundle like a giant tree protecting a nest of baby birds. Hannah tried to swallow past the painful ball of dread in her throat.

She knew that basket. She had bought it.

The distraught cries from the baby lying in the basket snatched her from the present and catapulted her back to a past she rarely dared to visit. She stared at that basket, its image becoming blurred by her tears. She fumbled back up the steps with trembling legs and knew with every ounce of her being and in every goose bump that taunted her arms whose baby that was. And what it meant.

Hannah took a deep breath and looked down into the

basket, struggling for control. She stumbled onto her knees before the baby, the stone steps tearing through her sheer nylons, but she didn't notice and didn't feel a thing because her eyes were on the baby. Pink blanket, pink fuzzy sleeper, pink hat; the ones she had picked out for her and given to her when she was born.

Emily.

Her skin was pale with blotches of red from her crying and the chill of the winter air. Hannah struggled to peel off her gloves with fingers that felt like rubber. She reached out and picked her up and felt a surge of relief when Emily stopped crying. Hannah held her close, with shaking arms, enveloping the infant in the folds of her coat. She rubbed the baby's back, nestling her own face into the tender spot of impossibly soft skin at the base of her neck. She took deep breaths and let the baby's angelic purity calm her.

Snow swirled around them as Hannah sheltered and warmed the baby. Minutes trickled by slowly, until Hannah finally stopped rocking Emily and looked into her wide, porcelain blue eyes wondering what had brought her here, but deep down she already knew. Louise was gone. Emily's mom was gone.

Hannah rose slowly, knowing she'd have to notify the police and knowing that she was going to have a hell of a battle on her hands with the child protective services office tomorrow. She wasn't going to play this one by the books. She had been there when Emily was born, and she was going to do whatever she could to make sure she didn't go through the foster care system.

She cradled the baby with one arm, ready to take out her BlackBerry and call her contact at the police station when she spotted something attached to the inside of the basket. She crouched down and read the note. It was scribbled on the back of a grocery receipt, in thick, black marker:

"I'm sorry, Hannah. I can't do this anymore. It's too hard. This life is too hard. Please find my brother, Christopher James. Please find Emily's uncle. He will raise her."

Acid burned her throat and Hannah fought the bile that threatened. This couldn't be happening. She had just spoken with Louise yesterday. *How had she missed the warning signs?*

Hannah held the infant closer to her chest. Emily's breathing became calm, her steady heartbeat a complete contrast to Hannah's erratic one. *What have you done, Louise?*

She buried her head against the baby's soft hair, and the tears that had been threatening finally triumphed for the heartache that Emily would one day face knowing that she'd been abandoned. She knew the depth of that pain. Hannah knew that kind of pain could never be erased.

Chapter One

"Have yourself a Merry Little Christmas…"

Hannah pounded the volume button on her car stereo so hard her index finger bent backward painfully. She rubbed her throbbing finger, glaring at the now black display. It was *so* not going to be a Merry Christmas. The odds were stacked against merry and highly in favor of miserable.

She had lied to her boss, co-workers, and broken some of the cardinal rules in child protective services to be here. While other people were decorating their homes, doing Christmas shopping, and attending holiday parties, *she* was sitting in a cold car, spying on a man from behind a snowdrift with a sleeping infant in the backseat.

But she'd finally tracked him down, and after three miserable, long weeks, she'd found baby Emily's uncle. Now all she had to do was knock on his door and introduce him to Emily.

Oh, and then convince him to adopt her.

Right. Great plan, Hannah.

If she had any sense of self-preservation she'd throw her car into reverse and hightail it out of Northern Ontario. She would brave the nightmare road conditions over convincing a man who had turned his back on his family for over a decade to drop everything and adopt his niece. But she knew she couldn't do that. Hannah turned in her seat to check on Emily who had been sleeping contentedly in her car seat.

Hannah glanced back at the rustic log cabin in front of her. She had everything rehearsed. She would approach the situation with compassion and honesty. She could *do* this. She *had* to do this. Hannah bit her lower lip as she peered through the peephole she'd created in her windshield. Her half-full cup of Starbucks holiday blend, long since abandoned, sat in the cup holder beside an empty baby bottle.

She ducked as she spotted movement in the house. Luckily, she was almost sure that the man hadn't noticed her silver Jetta buried in the snowdrift in the driveway. As soon as she had exited the highway and pulled out onto the back roads she'd felt like a moving snowman on wheels. When she finally found the cabin, located in *nowheres-ville*, she had drifted down the unplowed drive, saying a silent prayer she wouldn't hit the parked Range Rover.

Gurgling from the backseat jolted her. She had to go in before Emily woke up. *It's now or never, Hannah.* She turned on the engine one last time, blasting the heat on high before she had to leave the car.

She slipped her lucky red wool knitted hat with its oversized pom-pom onto her head with a decisive tug—she'd need all the luck she could get. She had a good ten minutes before she had to worry about Emily getting cold, but she added a few more layers of blankets onto the baby, who was already bundled in a bunting bag, hat, and mittens. Hannah reached over to the passenger seat, her hands blindly seeking out her purse and mittens, while her eyes stayed riveted on the cabin. She tucked the vintage Santa tin filled with homemade, sparkle-laden sugar cookies under her arm. No one could resist her Christmas cookies.

She hoped Louise's brother, once Christopher James, now Jackson Pierce, was the type of man to appreciate homemade cookies. His name change had added a few extra days to her search, but thanks to her friends at the police department and her own bit of ingenuity, she'd found him at this cabin. There was no trace of Christopher James when child services had looked for him, but Hannah knew the details of his past, and knew this man would want nothing to do with Louise's baby. She'd been pretty shocked by his identity. He was the founder and CEO of one of North America's largest computer software companies.

Hannah opened the door and the wind whipped snow onto her face as she struggled to get out quickly before the cold air infiltrated the car. She stepped into at least three feet of snow and fought the urge to yelp out loud as it made contact with her feet. *So much for waterproof boots.* Careful not to fall and drop the cookies, she walked as fast as she could, her feet feeling like lead as she reached the front porch. She glanced around the house and confirmed what she'd suspected from the inside of her car—there was no Christmas wreath on the door or Christmas lights. Or anything remotely Christmas-*y* at all.

It was an omen. A bad one.

She gave herself a mental shake, forcing herself to calm down. *Hurry up, Hannah.*

She took a deep breath of icy air and knocked. Her thick red mittens made it sound more like the paws of a furry animal thumping on the door…*maybe he couldn't hear the muffled knocking against the sound of the storm*. She was about to yank off a mitten when the door swung open. Her hand froze in midair, and the only thought she could process was why oh why did she have to be wearing the hideous red hat?

Jackson Pierce was at least six foot two inches of raw masculinity—the type of man who looked as though he belonged to no one, shared with no one. The kind that would normally make her run in the other direction. His hair was the color of expensive cognac, slightly mussed but clean cut, with eyes a few shades deeper. He was tanned, in that natural, not-from-a-tanning-salon sort of way, with dark stubble across a firm jaw and chin. Jackson was not what she expected.

Definitely built and definitely mouth-watering… *if you were into that sort of look.*

And she was *not.*

He frowned at her. "Are you lost?"

Hannah realized she must look like an idiot standing on his porch not saying a word. She lowered her arm, straightening her shoulders, and tried to project the image of the calm, cool, collected professional she usually was. "No, no. Not really."

In the six-hour car ride and the twenty minutes of stalking in her car outside, she'd had everything rehearsed. She had even practiced her speech in front of Emily and had earned a few enthusiastic gurgles. But now, in front of him, she couldn't bring herself to say the words she'd carefully planned. He raised his eyebrows, bracing his shoulder against the doorjamb. His fitted navy Henley shirt outlined his muscular arms and wide chest. The cold air obviously wasn't bothering him in the least.

"Do you need help?" *His voice.* Sort of like smooth silk and rough suede. Unfortunately, his carefully enunciated question also implied that he thought she was mentally challenged.

It was now or never. She cleared her throat and was sure to maintain eye contact.

"Are you Christopher James?" she blurted out, deciding

to use his real name at the last minute.

His brown brows snapped together. He pushed away from the doorjamb, and stood straight up. Suddenly he looked much more intimidating, and not at all nice.

"Who are you?"

"I'm Hannah Woods. Look, I'm sorry to bother you—" She took a deep breath. "I'm here because of your sister, Louise." Self-preservation was a skill she'd learned early in her life, and right now her instincts were telling her to run in the other direction.

"I don't have a sister."

Hannah cleared her throat. "I'm sorry. I know that—"

He scowled. "What? What do you know?"

"I know that you changed your name and—"

He slammed the door in her face and Hannah was in disbelief. She stood still and stared at the black door. One thing was for sure—Jackson Pierce or Christopher James or whatever his name was, was definitely not a Christmas sugar cookie kind of man. What had she been thinking anyway? That she could shove cookies down the man's throat while having a heart-to-heart about his sister and abandoned niece?

Tears began to blur her vision as she stared at the bare door, the reality of her situation setting it. Emily's temporary foster placement with Mrs. Ford would end soon and after that Hannah would have very little control over what happened to the baby. Hannah had fought vigorously to have the woman be Emily's interim guardian. Mrs. Ford was one of the best foster parents she'd ever come across. Hannah had gone to visit Emily every day after work. Spending time with the baby had become the highlight of her day. Hannah had been able to sleep at night, knowing the baby was in good hands while she searched for her uncle. It was Mrs. Ford's faith in her that allowed Hannah to take Emily to find her uncle without going through the child welfare office. There was no way Hannah's boss would have given her approval.

Hannah clutched the tin tightly to her chest and tried to ignore the lump in her throat that she suspected was due in part to feeling like a moron and in part to desperation. She would not cry. She did not cry. Before the night she'd found Emily, she hadn't cried in years. What was she going to do? The man she had gambled on was nastier than a man that good-looking had any right to be. And to top it all off, she was in the middle of nowhere during a blizzard with a two month old baby and only her car for shelter.

She squinted against the wind, looking at the car. She had to make a move and fast. She pictured little Emily being removed from Mrs. Ford's care. What if they didn't find permanent placement for her? Emily could have years and years of being shuffled around, never having a home of her own. Hannah knew all about that. She wasn't going to let that happen to this baby.

The minute she had picked up that baby outside the church she knew it was for a reason. Louise believed in her. And Louise believed in her brother. There had to be more to this man than what she'd just witnessed. She owed it to Louise. She had to honor Louise's wishes, no matter how miserable of a man Emily's uncle was. She couldn't chicken out now.

Hannah took a deep breath, straightened out her not at all fashionable hat, and knocked on the door again. She didn't know what she was going to say, but Jackson Pierce was not going to get rid of her that easily. Adrenaline and panic intertwined and wove their way through her body as she gave herself a mental pep talk. She wasn't a quitter. Emily needed her.

There was no answer.

She ripped off her mitten and pounded. Hard. But there

was still no answer.

Fine. Jackson Pierce thought he was stubborn? Well, he was about to meet his match. She lifted her foot and gave the door a swift, hard kick. Just as she was about to give it another one worthy of a champion soccer player, he whipped open the door. She struggled not to fall backwards as she almost lost her balance. She quickly lowered her foot, composed herself, and forced a smile on her face.

He didn't smile back.

"Look, Mr. Pierce, this is a matter of life or death."

He raised his eyebrows, clearly unimpressed. "Whose death?"

She frowned at him. "It's really a matter of life, actually."

"What's your name again?"

"Hannah, Hannah Woods." She was relieved by his more reasonable tone. The life or death line was always a winner at getting someone to take her seriously.

"Do you realize, Hannah Woods, that you are trespassing on private property?"

Okay, so maybe that line didn't work on Mr. Pierce. She felt her insides twist into a knot as she stared into hostile brown eyes.

She nodded carefully. "Yes, I realize that. I don't usually do this sort of thing, but your sister Louise died…"

He cursed loudly. "And let me guess, she left a pile of bills?"

She shook her head. She was about to explain when he cut her off.

"I don't associate with money-grubbing, junkie friends of my sister. So get your ass off my property and—"

"I'm not a friend of your sister's."

He leaned forward so that his face was a few inches from hers. "I don't care," he hissed. "I don't care if you were a friend of hers or a friend of the frickin' Pope. I. Don't. Care. So get the hell off my property."

He stepped back and this time he slammed the door so violently that she actually shuddered. It took her a few seconds to process what had happened.

Jackson Pierce was a jerk.

In all her imaginings about how this was going to unfold, him yelling at her and slamming a door in her face, *twice*, wasn't what she'd envisioned. She'd thought he'd at least hear her out. But he hadn't even given her a chance to tell him about Emily. She knew deep down, under that nasty temper, there had to be a good man. Louise had told her all about him, what a good brother he'd been. But that had been a long time ago, and Louise had made so many mistakes. He had obviously never forgiven her. When he hadn't been at the funeral Hannah assumed it was because he didn't know she had died. But now, after witnessing his palpable anger toward anything Louise, she wondered if he just hadn't cared to show up. So where did that leave Emily?

Hannah stood unmoving on the porch, the harsh wind hammering snow and ice up and down her body as though it too were taking a turn at trying to knock her down. Her car was already buried under the snow and must have lost most of its heat. She wasn't a quitter, but it was obviously time to think of a Plan B. She needed to get moving. But where the heck were they going to go at eight o'clock at night during a blizzard?

"Merry Christmas, Mr. Pierce," she grumbled to herself, as she carefully climbed down the porch steps, still holding her Santa tin filled with cookies. She could sit in her car and gorge herself on cookies until she came up with a plan. Luckily, she had two cases of baby formula in the trunk.

So much for the lucky hat. Maybe she should rip it off and then stomp on it. She was exhausted and cold and now, thanks to Jackson Pierce, miserable. She trudged through the snow as quickly as the wind and snow would allow, her sights on the car. Emily was going to need to eat again in under an hour, and the last thing she wanted to do was pull over in the middle of nowhere to give her a bottle. Maybe she could try and knock on the door of that charming bungalow at the end of the street—it had been adorned from top to bottom in Christmas decorations and lights. Surely, whoever lived there wouldn't turn a woman and a baby away in a blizzard.

What kind of a jerk would let a woman go out alone during a blizzard anyway?

• • •

What kind of a jackass yells in a woman's face and then lets her drive away in the middle-of-nowhere Northern Ontario, during a blizzard, at night?

Jackson looked out the window at the petite brunette as she tried to brush the snow off the windshield. But every time she did, the wind would blow on even more snow. By the looks of her, one strong gust might carry her away too. Even that grandma hat she was wearing was all white with snow.

He continued to stare out the window, his fists jammed into his jeans pockets. Guilt was ripping a jagged hole through his gut, as he recalled the shocked look in her eyes. He'd been an ass. He rarely lost his cool, and yet, a few minutes ago he stood yelling at this tiny slip of a woman at his front door. Would it be so bad to let this Hannah woman spend the night? How much of a threat could a woman who barely reached the top of his chin *with* the pom-pom be? He'd find out what she wanted and then make it clear that he had no intention of speaking to anyone about his family. Then tomorrow morning, when the storm was over, she'd leave. Easy. Done.

Jackson shook his head as she disappeared into a giant mound of snow. With a rough sigh, and a few of his favorite curses, he shrugged into his leather, sheepskin lined jacket and flicked on the outdoor lights. One way or another, women were always complicating his life. Even when he was trying to get away from them, they found him.

"Hey!" he called out, approaching her. The snow was past his shins and showed no sign of slowing. He squinted as snow and ice pellets beat into his face and eyes. She either couldn't hear him above the wind or she was purposely ignoring him.

She didn't bother to look at him when he reached her side. She kept brushing off the snow with angry bursts.

A cloud of snow hit him in the face. He wasn't so sure it was an accident.

"Look, you can spend the night here. Leave in the morning when the storm is over."

She paused and went back to fruitlessly wiping off the windshield with one arm, while clutching a round container like a football under her other arm. He spotted a Christmas wreath attached to the front bumper of her car. He tried not to groan out loud at the absurd ornament. He had never actually met anyone who went to the trouble of decorating their car for Christmas. She was working on her side windows, still ignoring him. Stubborn was the last thing he needed right now.

"Well, we both know you can't get anywhere with this weather tonight." He felt the ice pellets drumming against the back of his neck like a bunch of nails. She continued to pay no attention to him. Enough was enough. He walked over and grabbed the scraper from her hand. She glared at him and yanked it back.

"I'm *not* staying here. You're mentally unbalanced."

"What were you thinking coming here alone, at night? Obviously you intended on staying." He tried to pry the scraper out of her hand again, but it was as though that giant red mitten was super glued to the damn thing.

"Stop being a bully. I didn't think it would take me over six hours to drive up here. I *never* planned on staying here, so stop flattering yourself. I don't like you. I don't trust you. So leave me alone and let go of my brush!"

She yelled that last part and he let go, his hands up in the air in a surrender motion. He wasn't going to *beg* her to stay here.

Jackson watched as she fell backwards into a mound of snow. A tin flew in the air and what looked like cookies fell out. *Uh-oh.*

"My cookies!" She sputtered out and struggled into a sitting position in the snow.

He watched her collect the array of brightly colored cookies in the white snow and an odd feeling of regret came over him. *Of all the absurd...* Jackson felt he had no choice but to kneel down and help.

He cleared his throat, momentarily forgetting the cold. "Sorry, I didn't mean..."

"Save it," she snapped and he ignored the tears he thought he heard in her voice. *Not tears, please no.* He found a cookie and noticed with dread that it was shaped like a Christmas tree and covered with green sparkly looking things.

Jackson tried to place the ruined cookies gently in the tin, as though there was still some hope of salvaging them. She, on the other hand, tossed them in with a force that suggested she was royally pissed. At least she wasn't crying. Finally, she placed the lid over the round tin, banging Santa's happy face shut with her giant red mittens.

Jackson stood up and held out his hand. She glared at his hand and stood on her own. He shouldn't be surprised. He could have sworn he heard the word *jerk,* but with the howling wind he couldn't be sure.

"Sorry about the… cookies," he said awkwardly.

"Whatever. You're not exactly the milk and cookies type of guy anyway. You're more of the nails and arsenic type."

He had to stifle his urge to smile at her insult. The cookies had been for him. The fact that he had hurt her feelings was oddly unsettling. Added to that was the fact that she had baked for him. No one baked for him, unless of course they were paid to. He wasn't about to analyze his sudden sentimental reaction to a box of cookies. Besides, he wanted to get inside.

"Hannah, you can spend the night here."

She frowned up at him. "I'd rather sleep in my car."

Jackson gritted his teeth. It was damned irritating dealing with someone more mule-headed than he was always accused of being. Cookies or not, this was supposed to be his time away from stress…from civilization. This cabin was his anti-Christmas sanctuary, a place where there was no talk of family. No talk of Christmas. The only evergreens were outside and not one of them had a single damn light on them, just the way he liked it. But now he was being forced to harbor some strange woman who knew a hell of a lot about him and who had something to do with his sister.

He watched as she continued to brush the snow off her pants with one hand and hold that tin with the other. "Look, I'm not going to let you sleep in your car during a blizzard."

She stopped her swiping and cocked her head to the side. "Well, I guess you should have thought of that when you slammed the door in my face. It's not exactly the best way to make a guest feel welcome."

Jackson opened his mouth and then shut it, not knowing what to say. He was not a man used to being argued with. He had gotten used to the quick "yes, sirs" that he received from his employees.

She shot him a dirty look as she walked past him. He caught her arm. For a moment nothing happened and then she turned into steel beneath his grasp. Her eyes widened and she stared at him. He was trying to decipher the expression when she jerked her arm from his grasp. He noticed her breathing was shallow and rapid. That confidence she had shown only seconds before was gone. This woman felt threatened by him. His exes could say a lot about him, but violent was not an adjective used to describe him. He abhorred physical violence, and he'd never touched a woman in anger.

"I can't let you stay out here. I have a guest room," he said, trying his best to sound patient and calm.

She stared at him for another minute, then raised her eyebrows as she spoke. "Are you going to yell at me again?"

He shook his head sheepishly. He felt like he was being reprimanded like a small boy. Her face relaxed and she gave him a slight nod. "Fine. I've met crazier people than you and I know how to handle myself. I'll stay."

He stared at her incredulously. She'd called him crazy.

"On one condition," she said raising her chin and folding her arms.

"Condition?" She had barged in on his vacation and now she was negotiating terms of her stay?

She nodded once, the pom-pom bopping with the motion.

He gave a brief nod, why the hell not, it seemed he had very little control of the night anyway.

"No yelling in front of the baby," she said over her shoulder as she opened the back door of her car. Her head disappeared into the car and he stared numbly after her. Maybe he hadn't heard right, but then he heard an odd noise.

"Baby?" he finally managed to choke out through a throat that seemed to be filled with tar as she emerged from the car holding a baby seat.

Chapter Two

Hannah put on her best poker face as the wind whipped strands of her hair around her head while Jackson stared at her. She knew her knees were shaking and it was only partly due to the cold. Jackson Pierce had a stare that could send a man running. She saw his eyes shift to Emily's car seat. He couldn't see the baby because she had a pink blanket covering the opening.

"I don't yell at babies," he growled and shoved his hands in his pockets.

She shut her eyes briefly. She had done it. She had been given a second chance and she wasn't about to leave here tomorrow morning without some kind of a promise from Jackson.

"Do you have a bag or something?"

"Just my purse, diaper bag, and two cases of baby formula," Hannah called out over her shoulder, trying to sound pleasant. "Can you hold this a sec?" Hannah shoved the car seat towards his chest. He grabbed it with a grunt. The sooner he got himself acquainted with Emily the better.

Hannah poked around in her car, feeling Jackson watching

her. She retrieved her vintage holly and berry embroidered purse, quickly stuffing in a few of the books that had fallen out. She ignored his exaggerated sigh as she swung the loaded diaper bag over one shoulder. Then she walked around to the trunk, hauling out a box of baby formula.

"Do you, uh, want me to hold something for you?" Hannah almost smiled at the horror embedded in the strong lines of his face. He stared at all her bags, holding the car seat awkwardly.

"I'm okay."

"Follow in my footsteps, and hurry."

Hannah would have given him a salute had her hands not been full with all the baby gear. She got a tiny jolt of satisfaction by deciding not to tell him that he could have held the carrier by the handle, making it much easier. He glanced behind him a few times, no doubt making sure she hadn't fallen headfirst into a snowdrift. When they reached the porch he actually held the door open and waited for her to pass through.

Hannah walked into the house and quickly put down the heavy bags while Jackson closed the door against the harsh wind and they both stomped their feet on the sea grass rug, neither of them saying anything. The warm blast of heat comforted her, like she had walked into a friend's house, except Jackson's unsettling presence made it painfully clear that this was nothing of the sort.

"What should I do with this?"

"Oh here, I'll take her," Hannah said, slowly taking Emily's car seat and placing it on the ground. She crouched down and removed the blanket as Jackson watched. She never could stop the smile that came naturally whenever she saw Emily. The baby still slept soundly, bundled in her pink fuzzy bunting bag.

She jumped, startled, as a shaggy, excited dog came barreling over to her. Emily didn't even flinch.

"Charlie, sit." The dog answered with what appeared to be all of his self control as his tail wagged and thumped against the floor. Hannah laughed when he disobeyed Jackson and accosted her with unabashed licks and jumps when she held out her hand to him.

"Who is this?" She chuckled as she patted his clean but very messy fur.

"Charlie. My very undisciplined dog." Jackson shrugged out of his coat, the tension in his faced even more pronounced. Charlie wasn't exactly the type of dog she'd picture him owning. Jackson was more the Rottweiler type. She continued to study him. He was intimidating in that *I'm-so-confident-I-don't-have-to-be-nice* sort of way, with tight, pent-up hostility.

His features were rugged. His nose was perfect except for a bump that her years in social work told her had been broken once or twice. She could see how someone might want to punch him. He kept himself in peak physical shape. The broad shoulders were obviously thick with muscle and his wide chest easily outlined in the navy blue Henley shirt he wore. Not really the type of physique she'd expect for a computer guy. He was confident and arrogant, not a man to back down. Not the type of man she pictured with an infant. But Louise had been clear in her instructions and she obviously had faith in Jackson. Hannah had to remember that.

"Okay, Charlie, leave her alone." Jackson came over to brush Charlie away from her.

"He's very sweet," she murmured as Charlie settled down at her feet, still looking at her face as though he wanted to lap it up like an ice cream cone.

Jackson gave a terse nod, looking at the dog and not her. "He's got a good disposition."

"Have you had him long?"

"Almost ten years."

"He seems very friendly."

"He was a stray, a mutt. He found me and wouldn't leave me alone."

Her heart swelled. Wheels were spinning in her head. This was good. Very good. "Really? He was a stray?"

Jackson's eyes narrowed. *Oops.* She obviously sounded a little too ecstatic. She gave him a wan smile and took off her soggy mitts. She could tell he didn't know what to make of her reaction and he didn't want to expand his story about Charlie. It was still good news. Anyone who had enough compassion to take in an abandoned dog and adopt him couldn't be *entirely* evil. Okay, so Jackson was a little standoffish and obviously arrogant, but maybe all hope was not lost. If a shaggy dog could melt his heart, then surely an adorable little baby girl wouldn't be a problem.

"Let me take your coat."

"Sure, thanks." Hannah unbuttoned her coat and placed it in his outstretched hands, carefully avoiding any contact with him. She looked around the room while she pulled off her soaked boots. She was very aware of how cold her feet and legs were, and now that the snow on her jeans had melted, they felt like wallpaper paste had been plastered to her legs.

She looked around while he went to stoke the fire. A high peaked ceiling with wood beams made the room seem large, with a massive field stone fireplace as the focal point. A large, mahogany farmhouse table was in the center of eight chocolate brown leather armchairs, placed in a conversational formation in front of the fire. She had a hard time imagining him entertaining a large group of friends—or even one friend for that matter. But there was plenty of room for a baby. Hannah glanced over at Emily and made her a promise. *I'm*

*going to do this, Emily. I'm going to get your uncle to love you
and adopt you.*

• • •

Jackson poked the logs in the fire a little too harshly and
muffled his cough as a cloud of smoke engulfed his face. He
tried to appear calm and natural even though he felt like he'd
been backed against a wall by letting this woman and the baby
into his home. How had he gotten into this mess? He could tell
Hannah was trying to figure him out, and the look in her eyes
was unsettling, like she was pleased when he told her about
Charlie being a stray. He glanced over at her as she pulled off
her red hat and a mass of caramel colored hair came tumbling
out. He didn't want to notice how shiny and soft it looked. He
turned his attention to the fireplace again, but watched from
the corner of his eye as Hannah straightened out her clothing.

Hannah was definitely beautiful—not in a made up,
high-maintenance sort of way. She had high cheekbones and
full, rosy lips. And even though he didn't want to notice, her
eyes were like dark emeralds, large and almond shaped, with
impossibly thick black eyelashes. Even more perplexing than
their indisputable beauty was the emotion and the warmth
they held in them. They weren't vacant, they weren't flirty, and
they weren't the eyes of someone who had been friends with
his sister. They were clear and sharp, not hollow like someone
who was stoned all the time. No, she was too pulled together
to have been friends with Louise. So then who the hell was
she?

He willed himself not to look lower than her chin. *Dammit.*
Too late. She was curvy and slender in all the right places.
He felt himself fighting back a surge of complete and total
unwanted desire that gripped him out of nowhere. *What was*

going on with him? Must be a natural reaction to a woman who wasn't thinner than a twig. The last woman he'd slept with had been so skinny he wondered if she had ever eaten a carb in her entire life. But this Hannah woman was off-limits. He didn't date women with children or people associated with his family. And even though there wasn't a wedding band on her hand, she was probably with some guy. Not that it mattered. Not in the least, because he wanted nothing to do with her. Anyone connected to his family was the enemy.

"Look, I really am sorry for barging in like this."

She folded her hands in front of her and bit gently on her lower lip. Why were her lips to appealing? *Focus buddy, focus.* He shrugged, dragging his eyes away from her mouth. "Don't worry about it."

"I really wasn't planning on getting here so late—"

"How did you know I was going to be here? No one knows about this place except my business partner and PA." He saw the exact moment that her embarrassment turned to discomfort.

She waved a hand dismissively, but her voice sounded forced. "Oh, you can find anything online these days."

He crossed his arms in front of him. She wasn't looking so confident now. "No, you can't. You can't find anything about this cabin online."

She averted her eyes. "It wasn't her fault. I was probably a tad dramatic." Maybe it was the sudden change in tone or the softening of her expression that made him get defensive.

Jackson narrowed his eyes. "Whose fault?"

"I think her name was Ann," she said, biting her lip and looking away. Jackson tried to hide his shock. In all the years Ann had worked for him, she'd never released any personal details about him.

"What did you tell her?" He was genuinely interested in

knowing how the hell this woman had managed to get the address of his cabin.

"I may have said it was a matter of life or death."

He rolled his eyes. He was surprised Ann fell for that. "You seem to use that line as a catch-all, don't you?"

"Well, I really did need to find you. And she was quite concerned when I mentioned the death part," she said, lifting her chin. Something about the way she stood, the way she wouldn't stop looking at him made him uneasy.

But no matter what, he knew she was here to tell him something he didn't want to know. Not that it should matter. Nothing she could tell him would make him change his mind about his family.

He turned his back to her, focusing on the fire that didn't need his attention at all. He heard her shuffling around and then the quiet padding of her feet across the wood floor.

"I'm sorry to bombard you with this."

He ignored her attempt to open up the conversation. He turned to look at her, eyeing her snow-soaked pants. "Do you want to take off your jeans?"

Her green eyes grew comically large. "Pardon me?"

He almost laughed out loud at her expression. "I mean, you're soaked. I can get you a blanket or something and you can put your jeans in the dryer."

"Uh, no, I'll stand here for a few minutes. I'm sure they'll dry quickly by the fire." Her face was still red as she moved closer to the fire.

Why should he care if she wanted to stay in wet jeans all night? "Why don't I show you and uh—" He motioned to the baby with his chin. "—the baby your room?"

She nodded, but she bit on her lower lip. "Do you think I could have some hot water?"

"Hot water?"

"I need a small pot and some water on the stove to warm up a baby bottle. I can do it," she said, reading his confusion.

"No it's okay. I'll be right back."

• • •

Hannah stared at Jackson's back as he walked out of the room. Outside, she'd been sure he was an ogre, that she'd made the wrong call in trying to find baby Emily's uncle. But as soon as he told her the story of Charlie, she knew he had to have a heart underneath that cold exterior. And her instincts were never wrong. Now, all she had to do was chip away at him. She had less than twenty-four hours, but she could do it.

Once she'd found out his new name, information about Jackson had been easy. Jackson had started his own software company after graduating college, and he and his partner had turned it into a billion dollar company within ten years. His accomplishments were impressive, especially considering all he'd been through growing up. They shared a few similarities, not that he'd have any way of knowing that. She also knew that for all his success and all his money, he was notoriously private. So, her coming here declaring she knew things about his past must be disconcerting to say the least.

"Why don't I show you the guest room and find some things for you to wear while the water boils?" he asked, walking back into the room. The impact of his words and the fact that she was going to stay overnight with him caused a ripple of hesitation through her body. She was a confident, independent, successful woman, so why did he make her feel like she was an insecure, self-conscious fifteen-year-old? Because he was nothing like the men she was used to. Not that she dated much, but when she did, they were not the intimidating type. She gravitated towards men that weren't so tall, so built…so…

Jackson clearing his throat reminded her that he'd asked her something. *Right. Wear?* Was he going to offer her his clothes? Or did he have a stash from past girlfriends?

She forced a smile, trying to look her best to appear nonchalant, like she did this kind of thing all the time. "Yeah, that would be great."

He nodded and walked past her, down the hallway adjacent to the kitchen.

"Come with me," he said, not waiting for her. Hannah gave a quick glance to Emily and then followed him down the hall. There were three doors. Jackson passed the first room without saying anything and she assumed it was his. Hannah resisted the urge to peek her head in. From the looks of things around here, she could bet it was spotless. He stopped at the second door and Hannah pulled back abruptly before she walked into him.

"This is the washroom." He flicked on the light switch and Hannah looked inside. It was a spacious, square washroom, and looked as though it had been recently renovated, much like the rest of the cabin. Rustic, tumbled marble floors in a creamy, earthy tone were the backdrop to the large, freestanding deep soaker tub. A massive, sparkling glass shower enclosure, with a rain-shower head, looked as good as it had on the bathroom special she'd just watched on TV. A neutral marble counter with matching his and hers sinks sat atop mahogany cabinets.

Hannah's eyes settled on Jackson's razor and toothbrush on the counter. Seeing his belongings felt oddly personal, private.

"Does it meet your approval?"

Hannah forced a smile. "It's beautiful. Really, I'm sorry about how I intruded on you."

The half smile that had teased his lips fell slightly, and his dark eyes held a note of surprise. Hannah took a step back. She didn't know how they'd ended up standing so close, close enough that she could see the tiny flecks of cognac in his eyes, and the dark stubble on his face. And smell the fresh, woodsy aftershave he wore…

"And?"

"We honestly never meant to spend the night here."

"Whatever." He walked into the washroom and opened a dark drawer, pulled out a toothbrush still in its packaging, along with a square basket wrapped in clear cellophane filled with women's toiletries. He must have a lot of female guests.

"Help yourself to whatever you need, though I don't have anything a baby could want." He flicked off the switch and walked to the room next door without waiting for her to reply. He opened the next door, the one directly across from his, and felt for the light switch.

"This is beautiful." There was a king-sized mahogany sleigh-bed with a chocolate brown velvet duvet and matching throw pillows that looked so magnificent and comfortable that Hannah fought the urge to run over and sink into it. A stone fireplace was on the outside wall, with two leather armchairs in front of it accompanied by matching side tables and an antique rug.

"Thanks," Jackson said, walking past her and turning on the bedside lamp.

Hannah tucked her hair behind one ear. "You have good taste."

He smiled a patronizing, bored smile. "I had an interior designer do it."

Of course he did, Hannah. As if he would have spent weeks picking out fabrics for curtains and duvet covers. "Oh. Well. She, or whoever did a great job."

Hannah walked over to the bed and opened her purse. She felt like an idiot for letting her guard down and actually trying to have a conversation with him. Why couldn't he have been the stereotypical computer geek with pale skin, thick glasses, and scrawny body? Maybe if she started getting settled he'd get the hint and leave her alone for a few minutes, long enough to contact Mrs. Ford and let her know that she was going to be delayed.

"I'll get you some something to sleep in," he said, leaving the room.

A minute later, Jackson was beside her holding a folded navy blue T-shirt. "Here, it'll be a bit big, but it should be okay for one night."

Hannah took the T-shirt without looking at him and placed it on the bed. It was his. "Thanks."

"I'll be in the kitchen whenever you want that hot water."

"Sure," she mumbled. This was going to be the longest night of her life. She hoped Emily would sleep well tonight. She could use all the rest she could get.

"I'll let you get settled. There's a phone beside the bed if you need it. I'd use it sooner than later. I wouldn't be surprised if the phone lines go down. Cell phone reception out here gets a bit sketchy at the best of times."

"Great. I'll, uh, be a few minutes."

He walked out of the room without saying anything.

• • •

Jackson leaned against the kitchen counter, staring at the baby sleeping in the car seat. What he'd give for a night's sleep like that. He had moved her closer to the fire. Even a moron knew not to keep a baby by a door during a blizzard. He ran his hands through his hair, letting out a rough sigh. His evening had been going perfectly well until little-miss-smart-mouth crashed his annual *escape*-Christmas bash.

He glanced down at his watch. What was taking her so long? What if the baby woke up?

He decided she'd had more than enough time to get settled, he thought walking down the hall to her room. Besides, she was staying for one night, not a month.

He stopped himself from walking into her room. He heard her voice, her door slightly ajar. He would have knocked, but when he heard his name, he thought it might be wise to listen first.

"I found Jackson Pierce. I found little Emily's uncle. Thank you for letting me do this, Mrs. Ford. I'm so grateful… it's the weekend so no one from the child services bureau will be contacting you… yes… thank you. I'll call you when I know more… take care, Mrs. Ford."

Jackson stared at her back, trying to make sense of what she said, but that sick feeling he got whenever someone mentioned his family was lodged in his gut.

Jackson felt dread seep through his veins. *Emily? Emily's uncle?* As though she sensed his presence, Hannah turned around. Her bright green eyes loaded up with tears as they stared into his. *Her uncle. Her uncle.* Those softly spoken words echoed in his mind and they echoed in the beautiful face of the woman standing across from him. Jackson couldn't move, his body going cold as the truth of Hannah's visit sank in.

The baby.

That baby wasn't hers. It was his sister's.

Chapter Three

Jackson had heard everything.

The look on his face made her forget about Emily for a moment. All she could feel was the painful pumping of her heart and the acrid taste of the tears burning in her throat. This wasn't the way he was supposed to find out. She'd had a carefully rehearsed speech.

His eyes locked with hers and he strode across the room in what seemed like two steps. Suddenly there was no space between them, the room tiny and stifling. Panic set in.

"I want to know exactly who you are and what the hell you think you're doing. Everything. *Now*." His voice was raspy. Harsh. The anger that emanated from him was blatant. His jaw was clenched tight and the eyes that she thought were warm not too long ago, glistened with hate.

Hannah despised showing her hand. Hated showing that she was afraid of anything or anyone. Hated having someone know that she could be weak. But when he took a step closer to her, waiting for her answer, she took a step back, because he reminded her of a different man, of a different world, when she had no one, when she was helpless. But she wasn't that same girl anymore. She was a grown woman. She had confronted her demons years ago. She held her chin up and looked him squarely in the eye. *Don't show your fear. Don't show your fear.*

"I'll tell you everything you want to know, but I need you to back away from me and I need you to calm down," she whispered holding up a hand between them.

· · ·

He nodded slowly. "I am calm. I'm in control. I've never been out of control. I'm not going to touch you. I won't hurt you. I'm angry as hell right now, but I don't want you to spend another second thinking that you are being physically threatened by me. I've never, ever raised my hand to a woman." He was surprised at how gruff his voice sounded. He watched her try to figure out if she could trust what he was saying. She looked into his eyes and he could swear she saw things that he'd managed to keep hidden from those closest to him. He backed up a step and put his hands in his pockets, willing himself to look relaxed.

She finally gave him a small smile, and it tore at him, more than it should have. He barely knew her, but that expression on her undeniably beautiful face made his gut clench. It made him forget for a moment why he was so angry with her. For a second, the relief of her not being afraid replaced his rage.

She folded her arms in front of her and nodded. "Okay. Thank you."

"Don't thank me, for God's sake." Jackson ran his hands down the front of his face roughly, trying to stay in control of a situation that had the power to tear him down. He needed to get out of the room, away from her and everything she represented. He needed to gather his composure. He turned on his heel and walked out. When he reached the great room, Charlie came up to greet him, his scruffy tail wagging. Jackson patted the top of his head absently.

He heard her footsteps approaching.

"Jackson…" Her hesitant voice was barely audible against the wind and ice pellets drumming on the windows. He didn't really feel like turning around. He avoided looking anywhere but straight ahead because he was acutely aware of the baby asleep in the room. He did not want to acknowledge what or who she might be.

"I'm a child services worker." Hannah's voice halted his emotional auto-shutdown mode. He hadn't had to use that defense mechanism for a while, but it seemed whenever family was involved it was instinctual.

"Do you want a drink?" Right now, he was thinking he could down the whole bottle of his favorite whiskey.

He glanced over at her when she didn't reply. She shook her head. Her face was pale, but she didn't look afraid. He walked passed her to the mahogany liquor cabinet and poured himself a double shot. When he turned around, Hannah was sitting in front of the fireplace, her hands folded in her lap. His disloyal dog was contentedly sprawled across her feet. So much for man's best friend.

Jackson sat in the club chair opposite her. He stared into the fire, the cool crystal cradled in the palm of his hand, a contrast to the heat that raged through him. He took another drink and then spoke. "So, you're a social worker."

She nodded, turning her eyes away from the crackling flames to meet his. He read her expression easily and it made his tight muscles ease slightly. His gut told him that Hannah wasn't a liar. Unfortunately for her, he wasn't in the mood to mince words.

"I can't stand social workers."

He wasn't sure how she was going to respond to that one. A few seconds later she broke the silence. "So that means you've been let down by the system."

She obviously knew about his childhood. Yeah, he'd been let down. Abandoned. He didn't bother looking at her. "Every social worker that has ever come my way was completely useless to me. Full of empty promises and false hope. Hope is the last thing you give to kids who have nothing." The first time he told someone about the demented man who called himself a father he'd actually thought they might get help. Not for himself. If it were up to him he would have left, but his sister had refused to leave their home. So he stuck around for her. They lived in a dark, miserable hole of a house that reflected their father's state of mind. That man that had the power to strike terror with one look, to rule over them like a dictator, had destroyed his sister. But not him. Jackson had shut himself off emotionally, and then he grew. He grew taller and stronger until father and son stood nose to nose and the man that once thought he was so mighty learned to put his fists back in his pocket.

Hannah's soft, melodic voice clashed like lightning against the violence of his thoughts. "I know you don't know anything about me. This is a horrible way for me to approach you. I'm sorry that this is bringing you so much pain—"

"This is not bringing me pain." He hated that she was reading him, hated that she was right.

"You have to believe that I had the best of intentions. I had no choice. I risked everything to come here." Her words came out quickly and she sounded almost frantic, probably because she was scared he'd kick her out.

He took another sip of the whiskey and met her gaze. She was gutsy. He ignored the sheen in her eyes, the concern that he read in them. He didn't want to feel her compassion.

He clenched his teeth against it, as though he could make himself immune to it, but there was no going back now. She had trudged in here and hauled him back to a past he'd tried to forget. He'd deal with this now and then send her and the baby packing in the morning. He could deal with one tiny social worker and a baby and then go back to his scheduled life. He had his dog and his business. What else did he need?

He leaned forward in his chair, his forearms on his thighs, the cool, smooth crystal of the glass cupped tightly in his hands. "Why don't you tell me exactly why you are here?"

Hannah cleared her throat. "Your sister became one of my cases when she was pregnant. She was an addict who tried to stay clean for her baby."

Jackson felt his stomach churn with revulsion as a memory of his sister, strung out, falling into his arms, bulldozed him into the past again. He hated Louise's weakness. He hated that she hadn't trusted him enough to keep her safe. He hated that Louise had taken the easy way out. She had abandoned him and the reality of their lives in favor of mind-numbing drugs. She had sold her soul, her body, for a cheap fix. The sound of Hannah's voice reached in and brought him back.

"We found a group home for her and she did really well. She gave birth to a beautiful, healthy little girl that she named Emily."

Jackson stared straight ahead, avoiding her probing stare. *Don't look over at the baby.* She had named the baby after their mother, who had died when they were both children. When they were still friends. When they would tear through the woods bordering their home playing Batman and Robin until their mother would call them in for dinner, always with a smile, always with a home-cooked meal. That was all a long time ago. Such a different world that sometimes he wondered if it had happened at all.

He stared into his lap, seeing his mother's smile, so like his sister's. It was an image he rarely indulged in because if there was one thing that could bring him to his knees, it was the thought of his mother, of his sister, of what his life once had been. To him, that was weakness, and he abhorred weakness in himself and others. "I heard that Louise died. I didn't know there was a baby."

"You didn't go to the funeral."

"I didn't really think there was a point."

"She killed herself."

He nodded, ignoring the twisting in his gut. "I know."

"It came as a total shock to all of us. I found a baby on a church doorstep. *Her* baby. Emily. She was one month old. Your sister left a note to find the baby's uncle, Christopher James." He didn't have to look at her to know there were tears in her eyes.

Christopher James. *Chris*, as his mother and sister had called him. He swirled the whiskey in the glass, watching as the flames from the fire danced in the amber liquid. He knew no amount of the stuff would ease the pain. He had understood that nothing could ever take away gut-wrenching pain or sick memories. Louise hadn't learned that lesson.

Emily. His sister had a baby. *This baby*. Maybe she was better off without his sister. He knew first-hand blood meant nothing when that person was a substance abuser. He had learned that the hard way. Jackson looked up at Hannah. "What about the baby's father?"

Her green eyes were filled with pain that couldn't be false. A part of him hated that—hated that the compassion and pain were so genuine. And a tiny, tiny part of him that didn't want to acknowledge it felt comforted by her.

Hannah shook her head. "She didn't know who the father was. You are Emily's only relative. You are documented as her next of kin."

He needed to shut this down before she got crazy ideas into her head. "So what do you want from me? To sign some papers—?"

"I want you to adopt her." Jackson felt like someone had ripped his insides out with one hard tug. It was ridiculous. Absurd. It was one thing to inform him that he had a niece, and quite another to expect him to adopt her.

"Are you kidding me?" He bit back the profanities that he thought were missing from that statement to try and keep this civil.

She shook her head slowly.

He was speechless. She actually wanted him to keep his sister's baby. The sister who turned on him, betrayed everything he'd ever done for her and tried to ruin him. He turned away from Hannah in disgust. Hannah was responsible for bringing all of this to him. He hadn't asked for this crap. He should have let her drive away. *Adopt a baby*. It was so insane, the idea of him taking in a baby, that he didn't even try and process it.

"Jackson?" He heard the concern in the soft voice that tried to coax him into speaking. He knew exactly what she was doing now. She wanted him to talk, to open up. Fat chance in hell. His muscles tensed even tighter. He stared into the fire. "You don't know anything about me. I run a company. I work twelve hours a day and live in a penthouse in downtown Toronto. I don't know anything about babies. *I don't want a baby*."

It didn't faze her. She folded her hands on her lap and stared at him levelly. "She is your flesh and blood, Jackson. It was your sister's last wish."

"My sister was a junkie. I offered her help hundreds of times and she refused. If she wanted what was best for her baby she would have taken the help being offered and sobered up. Blood ties mean nothing to me."

She nudged her chin toward his drink. "I changed my mind. Could I have a glass of whatever you're drinking, please?"

He was surprised by the request. He nodded, walking across the room. A moment later she accepted the snifter of whiskey and took a sip while he sat down. He didn't want to be impressed that she didn't cough as she swallowed.

"I know you didn't have a good relationship with your sister, but Emily is just a baby," she said leaning forward.

He shrugged and ground his teeth together. This was not his problem, no matter how hard she tried to make him think it was.

She frowned at him when he didn't answer. "She'll be placed in foster care if you don't adopt her."

He tried not to feel anything, especially the ugly emotions that had consumed him for years. The bitterness, the anger... no, he wanted to continue feeling nothing.

• • •

Hannah crossed her legs in front of her nervously and watched as Jackson digested that last piece of info. She tried not to panic. It didn't look as though she got through to him at all. The only sign she had that he processed what she said was the rigid, tense lines in his body. If she completely angered him, she'd ruin her chance at getting him to agree to this. But if she stopped now, he might not let her broach this again and tomorrow she was leaving.

"The foster care system is a place for children who don't have any family capable of caring for them. Your sister thought she could trust her daughter to you." Hannah would have given anything to have been adopted by some long-lost relative who had come forward to rescue her, to know that she was connected to someone.

She held her breath. He looked into the bottom of his empty glass and then up at her. "Well, I'm sure there's lots of great people out there who want a kid."

"There are, but there are also no guarantees. And in the meantime she'll be in foster care. You don't know where she'll end up—"

"It's not my problem. If my sister wanted me to have anything to do with this baby she would have contacted me when she was born."

"She said she'd tried so many times in the past, but that you refused to see her. After Emily was born, I think something happened. She became fragile again. I don't think she could have handled your rejection." Hannah couldn't filter out the accusation from her voice. She had her own guilt to work through for not noticing any signs that Louise was failing, but her brother did too. Hannah knew she was too emotionally close to this case, but her past collided with baby Emily's and she was desperate to honor Louise's wish.

He scowled at her. "Did she tell you that after I spent years protecting her she bailed on me? That I searched for her and tried to help her? That she and her addict friends broke into my house and trashed it, stealing everything of value I had? That I almost lost everything when I started out because I trusted her?"

Oh, Louise had told her all right. When Louise had been sober she'd confided so many things to Hannah. And whenever she spoke of her older brother her voice had been filled with such pain. She had stopped seeking him out after that night of the break-in. She'd told her of their childhood— before and after their mother had died.

Hannah stared at the handsome, strong lines of Jackson's face and tried to picture the fun-loving, energetic boy that Louise had described. She tried to see the teen who had always stepped in to defend his sister against their father. The one who took beatings to spare his younger sister. And she could see it, she could see the boy that had become stronger, taller, and had finally been able to overpower their father. She could see all of that—Jackson was strong and loyal. If he felt that need to protect his sister at one time, surely he would do it for her innocent baby.

Hannah placed her empty glass on the side table. "Your sister had a lot of regrets. How your relationship ended up was her biggest. She was humiliated. Louise said as soon as she got her life together, she was going to try and reconnect with you. She was devastated by how she treated you. You were her protector." Her voice trailed off as she watched his jaw clench and unclench. She could tell he struggled with his control. Jackson finally broke the silence, his voice harshly tearing through the calm.

"It's a little late for regrets, isn't it?"

"You can't change the past. Your sister is gone, but you have a niece who needs you. Emily hasn't done anything wrong. It's not her fault that her mother killed herself."

Hannah watched his lip curl into a smile that tried to appear mocking, but the pain was etched on his face so strongly that Hannah could almost feel it herself.

"No, and it sure as hell isn't my fault either. She'll be better off with someone who wants a child."

Hannah squeezed her sweaty palms in her lap. "It doesn't work that way. No one magically gets placed with the world's best parents. She needs *you*. You are her uncle. She needs someone tied to her past. She needs someone her mom trusted. What better person is there?"

Jackson tilted his head back and she studied the strong line of his jaw and neck. He squeezed his eyes shut. "I don't want her baby."

"Stop thinking of yourself."

He jerked his head around to meet her eyes. She could read the surprise in his eyes—and the anger.

Hannah concentrated on the sounds of the crackling fireplace and Charlie's soft snore. The tension in Jackson's frame was contagious. The air felt hot and prickly.

"You think a bachelor who has never even held a baby is a good choice for a father—the man that abandoned his family and changed his name to forget them? I turned my back on my sister. I refused to see her, I refused to talk to her." He finished off the rest of his whiskey with a sharp swallow. Hannah felt the pain of his regret, even if he wouldn't admit to it. It was embodied in every tightly wound muscle in his body, in the lines in his face. He regretted what had happened with Louise and that gave Hannah hope that there was still a chance. She wanted to tell him everything—about her past, about the other reason she wanted him to adopt Emily. But she couldn't talk about that and stay detached. She was already in way over her head.

"You are her *uncle*."

"Stop saying that."

Hannah looked into his eyes and then nodded. "Louise made mistakes, Jackson. Her baby shouldn't have to suffer for them."

"Why the hell do you care so much anyway?"

She clenched her hands to keep from shaking. "I don't want her to enter the system," Hannah whispered, almost choking on the words. She squeezed her eyes shut for a moment, trying to block the image of handing over that baby to some foster family, not knowing what would happen to her.

She had broken a cardinal rule—she had gotten too close to Louise and Emily. She wouldn't be able to keep Emily safe once she left Mrs. Ford's. She wouldn't have unlimited access to her like she did now. She held her breath as she waited for him to say something. It was obvious he didn't want to hear what she said. "You'll regret it," she said softly, forcing herself to walk over to him on legs that felt like jelly. She watched his jaw clench at her words. She felt the heat of the fire on her face, the flames attacking the pile of logs, the strength of the fire burning any hope she had of Jackson agreeing to this.

But she had to tell him. "This decision will haunt you. It won't erase your past and it definitely won't take away your pain. Emily will be gone, but that anger, that resentment you feel toward your sister won't go away. It'll eat away at you until you're not the same person anymore. You'll be going about your life and then you'll stop every now and then and wonder what happened to that little baby. You'll wonder if someone is looking out for her the way you did for Louise. You'll wonder if the system failed her the way it failed you."

"Enough!" He growled into the fire, sounding more like a wounded animal than a man. Hannah didn't move, didn't breathe. He finally turned to look at her, his brown eyes dark and void.

"You don't know a damn thing about me, Hannah. I don't know what the hell made you think you had the right to come here and find me, but that was your first mistake. You don't know a damn thing about my life, so don't apply your ideals to me. Tomorrow, when the road gets plowed, go home."

Chapter Four

Hannah tried not to let her smile waiver as Emily drifted off to dreamland. She decided that a smile should be the last thing Emily saw before she went to sleep.

Emily sighed deeply, made a little sucking motion with her rosebud lips, and finally succumbed to a deep slumber. Hannah held on to her smile for a second longer before reaching for her phone. She needed to call Allison. She knew her best friend and fellow social worker would be out of her mind with worry. Seconds later her friend's voice greeted her on the other end of the line.

"Allie? It's me," Hannah whispered into the phone.

"Oh my God! I've been calling you for the last four hours!"

"I know, I know, reception has been sucky, I'm sorry—"

"Why would you have bad reception? You live down the street from the office."

Hannah cleared her throat, preparing for the onslaught she was about to endure from her friend. "Well, I'm not exactly in Hope's Crossing right now."

"Oh my God, you didn't—"

"I did. I'm here."

"Hannah, I thought I talked you out of that crazy idea. You could be charged with kidnapping."

"Mrs. Ford signed off on me taking Emily up here."

"Fine, but what about Jean? She's going to chop you up and kick your butt out of the department." Jean, their boss, played everything by the book. She hated that Hannah took chances and resented that Allison wasn't afraid of using her contacts and friends to help a child. Allison had helped Hannah out more than once, so Jean had it out for both of them.

"Not if I get Emily's uncle to adopt her. I had no choice, Allie. You know that. I screwed things up with Louise. The least I can do is make sure Em is placed with her uncle," Hannah said, sitting on the large bed.

"What happened to Louise wasn't your fault. I know you were close to her and I know your history, but you've put everything on the line here. Louise wouldn't blame you for backing down."

"Not going to happen," Hannah said, staring at Emily. Hannah had made a makeshift bed for the baby beside her, careful that it wasn't too soft and that she couldn't fall off.

"Have I ever told you you're the most stubborn person I've ever met? I will do everything on my end to hold off the witch-hunt. So, you've met Louise's brother? And I'm assuming he's met Emily?"

Hannah fidgeted with the hem of the long shirt Jackson gave her to wear. "Technically yes, we've all met."

"What do you mean technically met?"

Hannah glanced over her shoulder, and lowered her voice. "Well…"

"What did he say? Will he do it?"

No. And that crushed her because every now and then

during the evening with him she would catch glimpses of the man she thought he might be. But everything that came out of his mouth contradicted that. Maybe she was a dreamer, a hopeless romantic who wanted to believe that the reclusive, handsome billionaire would drop everything to save his innocent niece. But Jackson wasn't like that at all. Scratch that. He *was* handsome, more than he deserved to be considering his attitude. And he *was* a self-made billionaire, which again made things even worse because that meant he had drive, talent, and brains.

"Hello, what did he say? Is he going to adopt her?"

The image of Jackson Pierce telling her to get the hell off his property sprang to mind. "He hasn't exactly agreed yet," Hannah said, wishing her phone would lose reception.

"He said *no?*"

"It was just shock talking, I'm sure. Listen, I'll call you when I'm on my way back. The weather is brutal out here, so I'm stuck for the night. But he's a great…" Hannah tried not to choke on her lie. "…a great host and we'll be fine. Oh dear, I think Em is waking up. I'll talk to you later, Allie. You're the best."

"Hannah," her friend groaned. She could just picture her blue eyes filled with worry.

"Bye," Hannah whispered, not giving Allison a chance to ask any more questions. Hannah hoped to hell some sort of a miracle would happen between now and tomorrow morning.

In the crisp, bright morning that would surely follow the blizzard, maybe he'd have some sort of awakening… An odd noise interrupted the droning sound of the wind outside. She glanced over at Emily. It wasn't her. What was it?

She paused, listening.

Just wind.

Then she heard it again. It came from the hallway. Her

heart started pounding and she swung her legs over the side of the bed. Her bare feet padded across the room and she stopped at the door and listened again.

Nothing.

She opened the door slowly and peered into the hallway. Everything was dark except for the small bedside lamp she'd left on in her room. Jackson's lights were off. She flicked on the hallway light and tiptoed close to the great room… and then she heard it, a mumbling, almost a groan. She turned around and walked to stand outside Jackson's room. It was definitely him.

Her palms started sweating as she contemplated what to do. It wasn't like they were friends. In fact, his last words *had* been to get the hell out of his house tomorrow. She couldn't just walk into his room and intrude. But then again, if he was sick, wasn't it her duty as a human being to help him? And she *was* a social worker. Wasn't it her job to help people? She bit her lower lip, her right hand on the doorknob. *Okay, Hannah, if you don't hear anything for another minute leave and go to your bedroom. If you hear him again you've got to walk in.*

Sure enough, a few seconds later she heard him again. She took a deep breath and slowly opened the door, the floorboards creaking as she walked across the threshold. She held her breath but didn't move. The room was dark so she opened the door fully, letting the light from the hallway cast enough of a glow so that she could see where she walked. Jackson was in bed. A dark duvet was thrown off his body and he lay on his back, his head turned away from hers.

The one thing she could make out clearly was that Jackson only slept in boxers. And every inch of his long frame was solid and muscular. That strength that was so obvious, even while he slept, made her slightly nervous. After their time together and his words about never touching a woman in anger, she believed him. She did trust him in that respect.

She watched him for a few more seconds. She really should stop staring. Honestly, it wasn't like he was the first beautiful man she'd ever seen. Okay, well, maybe the most beautiful man she'd ever seen. *Snap out of it, Hannah.* It was an invasion of his space, and he looked fine now.

She started to tiptoe out of the room, wincing as each creak in the floor sounded louder than the storm outside. She had almost made it to the open door when a guttural cry that sent shivers down her spine tore through the room. She whipped her head around to look at Jackson. He still slept. His eyes were shut. She could make out the pain in his features, and she saw the sweat lining his forehead. He was having some sort of nightmare.

She had to wake him up, but that would mean getting close to him. What if he lashed out at her without realizing what he was doing in his sleep? Or when he woke, he could be horribly upset that she'd intruded. She couldn't stand here and do nothing.

Her eyes scanned the room frantically and then settled on a stack of books on his bedside table. Maybe she could nudge him awake with a book. A hardcover. At least she'd be able to keep a little bit of a distance, and she wouldn't have to touch his bare skin. Perfect.

When she saw him clench the sheet, his forearm and hand rigid with strain, she finally moved. She quickly grabbed the top book on the stack and moved beside him. She bit her lower lip and tapped him on the shoulder with the book. Then she quickly stepped back, almost tripping over her own feet.

Nothing. He still didn't wake up.

She inched forward again, holding her breath, book in hand and plunged it into his shoulder. Suddenly a hand that felt like steel clamped down hard on her wrist and yanked her onto the bed, flipping her over and pinning her on her back. Jackson's strong, muscular legs straddled hers and locked her arms down beside her head. She stared into his eyes and knew he wasn't quite awake. She stayed perfectly still, her heart pounding painfully in her chest, waiting for him to become aware of what he was doing.

"Jackson."

His eyes went from blankness to reality. He swore loudly and ducked his head, pushing off of her and rolling onto his back beside her on the bed.

Hannah lay still beside him. She tried to catch her breath but couldn't move yet. Her body felt like a quivering mass of gelatin.

"Sorry, I didn't know what I was doing. I didn't know it was you," Jackson said a moment later, his voice raw and gruff. "Are you okay?"

Hannah struggled to regain her composure. She glanced over at him, his rigid posture unmistakable in the dim lighting. "I should be asking you that."

He ran his hands over his face roughly. "I sometimes have, uh, nightmares."

"I heard you from my room, I thought you were sick or I never would have come in here," she said haltingly, not knowing if he was angry with her.

"God, I never meant to scare you." He squeezed his eyes shut, before turning to look at her. Hannah felt her heart jolt unexpectedly at the softness in his voice. He wasn't angry at all. He wasn't the same man in front of the fire yelling at her to go home. She looked into his eyes and saw how soft and warm they could be. She noticed the shape of his lips. They were sensual, perfectly shaped. He had turned on his side so that he faced her completely. She was still on her back, there was no way she'd turn too… it was too… intimate.

When she lifted her eyes to meet his she saw that he was still looking at her. She remembered he had asked her if he had scared her. "You didn't. I'm not afraid of you," she finally answered, her voice sounding strange to her ears. "Besides," she said, forcing herself to sound flippant, "I've taken lots of self defense classes. I could have tossed you to the ground with one foot if I needed to."

The sound of Jackson's deep laughter filled the room and made her smile involuntarily in the darkness. He had a rich and deep laugh. She didn't want to notice that either.

"I'll be sure to remember that," he said, the smile still in his voice.

They were whispering in the darkness. The intimacy of the situation was not lost on her. His body was so close that she could feel the warmth emanating from him. She could smell his soap combined with his own masculine scent, and she found herself responding to him in a way that was anything but platonic. And that was not a good idea. She frowned down at her clothes. Both of them were wearing far too little clothing for two people who barely knew each other. She needed to get off the bed pronto.

"You're sure I didn't hurt you?"

She nodded frantically as she watched his hands move to gently grasp her wrists. He looked them over. She *couldn't* say anything because she had lost her voice. His hands were warm, large, and a delicious, molten heat began swimming through her as he held on. His thumb grazed the soft, velvety underside of her wrist and the innocent touch felt anything but. She quickly slipped her wrists out of his hands, needing her body to not be in contact with his, but she wasn't prepared for the loss she felt at not having him touch her. Not good. And there was no way she was going to acknowledge the meaning behind the fact that he was the first man she found herself wanting to touch her since… a long time.

"You didn't hurt me." Why did her voice have to sound so breathy? She couldn't break his gaze. The air was warm and like a cocoon, capturing them in a false sense of familiarity. She needed to get out of the room and away from an enticingly half-naked Jackson. Because right now, more than anything, she wanted to reach out to touch his bare skin. She was drawn to him and she shouldn't have been. As soon as she got back into the safety of her own room she was going to list each despicable trait the man had and then do a personality comparison list to Ebenezer Scrooge. That should sufficiently deal with any sort of misplaced desire she had.

"I'm still sorry." He braced himself on his forearms, watching her closely. She could make out the lighter shades of cognac in his eyes, and the softness, the warmth was still there. She didn't say anything. Couldn't. She should be concentrating on the list.

"It was no big deal."

"Thank you."

"For what?" Why had she asked that? Why wasn't she moving? *Get off the darn bed, Hannah.*

"For waking me up." His eyes fell to her lips and she felt a heat bloom from deep within her. Then his gaze wandered up to her eyes and traveled the length of her body. Suddenly she felt like she wore absolutely nothing. She tugged roughly at the T-shirt to cover a little more of her exposed legs. And then he smiled again, a sort of sexy, satisfied grin. The kind that told her he knew exactly why she was so uncomfortable, and that he liked it.

She needed to get out of here. Again, her body wasn't getting the message her brain was frantically communicating, so she didn't move.

"Hannah?"

"Yeah?"

"Why did you come here, really?"

She turned to look at him. "Here? Like your room?"

He shook his head. "The cabin."

She frowned at him. "I told you, I want you to adopt your sister's baby."

He nodded and shrugged gently. She refused to be taken in by the display of muscles that that one little move caused to ripple through his upper body. *Concentrate.*

"I know, you said that, but you can't possibly do this for all your cases. You drove through a blizzard. You tracked down a guy who changed his name, which you must've pulled a hell of a lot of strings to do. This goes beyond job dedication, don't you think?"

She stared up at the ceiling, trying not to reveal any emotion. She couldn't exactly explain something that she'd barely figured out herself. "I feel responsible, you know? I got to know your sister. I never thought she would have—" She paused for a moment. "Killed herself and then when I found Emily on the church doorstep, I—" She tried to hide the emotion in her throat but couldn't control the catch. "I knew I had to do what's best for her. I brought her home that night and held her. She's this tiny, perfect, innocent little girl. She deserves the best, not to be cast aside and left with strangers. She needs someone to protect her, to give her a wonderful, happy childhood." She stopped talking because she wouldn't be able to hold back her pain anymore, or the rest of the truth. Lying in his bed like this made her realize how much was missing from her life. In the darkness of the night, in the warm shelter from the storm, the enigmatic man beside her made her yearn for so much—someone to speak with in the dead of the night, someone to share a bed with.

"I should go… to sleep."

He grabbed her hand. She didn't want to turn and look at him. She took a steadying breath and channeled that self-control that she'd perfected years ago.

"You completely caught me by surprise," he said slowly. She didn't know if he meant her or the news about Emily. When she raised her eyes to meet his, they were filled with a desire she didn't want to acknowledge. She stood quickly, still holding down the hem of the T-shirt. She walked as fast as she could to the open door, the floorboards creaking as loudly as the beating of her heart. She needed to get to work on that list right away.

"Hannah," he called out, his voice carrying a hint of amusement.

She turned to look back at him, trying to look calm, cool, and collected. Do not look below his chin. *Do not look at the display of muscles and abs, Hannah.*

"Yes?" She cringed at the high-pitched sound of her voice. She sounded like the chicken she began to resemble.

"Did you *poke* me with a book?"

Chapter Five

The storm wasn't over.

The roads weren't getting plowed.

Hannah and the baby weren't going home today.

Jackson leaned forward, bracing his hands against the marble kitchen counter. It was so dark and windy that it barely looked like morning. Even if he had wanted to enforce what he'd said about her going home today, there was no chance. The weather wasn't showing any signs of relenting.

After Hannah left his room last night, he'd felt the distinct, and very unexpected, sensation of loss. He wasn't angry anymore. He knew what it must have taken for someone like her to enter his room, especially considering how the evening had ended with him telling her to go home. He'd seen the fear and felt the trembling in her body when she'd been under him. And the feel of her in his arms led to a whole other set of problems. His attraction to her was undeniable, and it was beyond physical, which was entirely new for him. He admired how gutsy she was, despite whatever issues she had with men. She had driven hours through a blizzard to confront a stranger. Hell, that took courage.

He was about to get himself some coffee when he heard soft footsteps approaching the kitchen. He turned around at the sound of her hesitant hello, and his gut clenched. God, she was beautiful. Her hair tumbled around her shoulders and he remembered how soft it had been against his bare chest last night. The curves of her body intimately pressed against his wouldn't be forgotten for a long time.

"Morning," he said. He smiled and saw the tension leave her face. Who knew what she thought of him? That he'd send her on her way in a blizzard or yell at her?

"I made a pot of coffee. Want a cup?"

"Please," she said and walked in a few more steps.

"Have a seat," he said. He handed her one of the pottery mugs his designer had chosen, motioning to the kitchen table. She sat opposite him, tucking one leg under her. She added milk to her cup and then looked up at him. She had gorgeous eyes, large and clear. And warm. The kind of eyes that made you think you could tell anything to this woman and that she'd understand, and wouldn't judge. He gave himself a mental shake. He needed to be nice, that was all.

"I'm sorry about last night. And obviously, I don't expect you to leave today."

She took a sip of her coffee, wrapping her hands around the oversized cup. She had delicate hands. Her nails weren't long, but nicely shaped. They didn't have a French manicure or god-awful loud color on them... wait a second, when the hell did he even look at a woman's hand... other than to see if there was a wedding ring on it? She looked into her cup. She hadn't said anything yet and he realized that he was anxious for her response. Anxious in that sort of way that told him he cared about her feelings. Crap. First the nails, now the feelings.

"I was kind of worried about how we would get back in this weather," she said with a twinkle in her eye, her lips curling up into a deliciously alluring smile. He needed a drink, but it was way too early in the day for that.

"Look, let's call a truce okay? I think I've already made it clear that your plan doesn't really...work for me. If we talk about it again, we're going to end up arguing. You've got to understand that I have no intention of ever going along with this."

The warmth in her eyes disappeared and was replaced by a fiery sheen. Hell, she probably had as big a temper as he. Her full lips were pinched and thin, and he bet she held back a long string of curses. Too bad. He got up and rummaged through the cupboards, aware that she was watching him, fuming. "What would you like for breakfast?" He forced himself to sound nonchalant.

"How about a knife? You can stick it right through my heart."

He didn't know if he wanted to laugh or groan with frustration. He was going to ignore the bait. "It must be hours since you've eaten. Is cereal okay? I have muffins too."

"Not hungry."

He turned around to look at her. Her leg was crossed over the other and she drummed her fingers against the table. He sighed. "No point in starving yourself because you're pissed at me."

She raised her eyebrows.

"Fine. I'll heat up a muffin. Lemon cranberry," he said when she continued to stonewall him.

"*You* bake?"

He shook his head, insanely relieved that she was speaking to him again. "My housekeeper does. She freezes a bunch of stuff for me to bring when I come up here."

"So you have a lot of help at home?" she asked, looking innocent. She folded her hands neatly in her lap. He already knew her better than that.

"I'm a busy man. I work late hours. Very late. Not *family* man type hours," he said, enunciating every word to make it clear that he knew exactly what she was getting at. The microwave beeped and he set the muffins in front of her. He sat down and waited for her to take a muffin before grabbing one himself.

"Ah, so you have everything then."

He gave a terse nod.

"You have money, a penthouse, a company, a cabin," she said, popping a piece of the muffin into her mouth

"Yes."

"I mean, what more could there possibly be in life other than money, assets, and work?" She put another piece of muffin in her mouth and he lost his appetite. Who was she to judge him?

The sound of a baby's cry prevented him from making a retort. Hannah jumped up, pulled out a bottle from the fridge, and dropped it in the small pot already filled with water on the stove. The baby. That baby was his niece. His sister's responsibility. Not his.

He stood up so fast his chair nearly toppled over. "Do you mind if I go do some work?"

He could tell she was surprised at his abrupt interruption. She shook her head and licked her lips again. Yeah, he was so outta here. He refilled his cup of coffee and walked out of the kitchen.

· · ·

Hannah laughed as she placed Emily into the bathroom sink. The baby loved her baths and gave a delighted gasp as her body made contact with the warm water. Hannah cradled her head with one hand and rubbed the soapy washcloth over Emily's soft skin. Emily kicked her legs and gurgled loudly. She yelped as Emily splashed her.

"Everything okay in here?"

Hannah turned her head as Jackson walked in wearing an expression she couldn't quite figure out. He looked down at Emily and for a second she thought he was going to smile, but instead she saw his jaw clench. She tried not to let her disappointment show. She didn't expect him to be reduced to a pile of mush by looking at the baby, but maybe a hint of a smile…

"We're doing fine," she said as she rinsed the soap off Emily's slippery skin. "Every time I give Emily a bath I seem to get soaked."

She busied herself with getting Emily out of the water and into the waiting towel, and pretended not to be aware of Jackson's intense gaze. His silence was disconcerting. She almost preferred the sarcastic comments to the silence. She spotted the sleeper that she'd already laid out peeking out from under the towel. Almost positive Jackson hadn't noticed, she slipped it into the sink.

"Oh shoot!"

"What is it?"

She avoided eye contact and focused on the now drenched sleeper while keeping Emily bundled in the towel.

"Her sleeper is soaked! Here," she said and shoved Emily into his arms. "I'll be right back. I'm going to grab a new one." She didn't bother waiting for a response and ran out of the washroom, her heart beating as though she'd just committed a felony. She was such a bad liar, she thought as she rummaged around for the only other sleeper she had. She waited a few moments before walking back into the washroom. Would Jackson's heart melt by holding his little niece?

He awkwardly cradled Emily in his arms. Was he smiling at her? Was he choked up with emotion?

Jackson looked up as soon as she approached his side and for a second she could have sworn she saw something warm in his expression. But then he handed Emily off to her and strode out of the room without saying anything.

Hannah stared into Emily's wide blue eyes. So much for her plan.

• • •

Jackson told himself that all babies were cute. Emily was not a special baby. Human adults were biologically programmed to respond to babies. It was how the human race propagated. His wanting to keep holding the baby was only natural. And the connection he felt when he stared into those wide, curious eyes was completely ridiculous. That was that. A figment of his imagination. He needed to get down to work and count the hours until Hannah and his… the baby left.

He settled himself at the table in the great room and opened his laptop and briefcase. He came out here every year not to escape work, because he loved work and he loved the company he'd built with his best friend. No, he came out here to escape a season filled with year after year of bad memories. Here, there was no pressure to act like Christmas meant something more to him than any other day on the calendar. Until, of course, Hannah came crashing into his world.

He pretended to be deep in concentration at his computer an hour later when he heard Hannah enter the room. She had that giant bag that looked ready to burst with books sitting on her shoulder along with a fresh mug of coffee. He ignored the smell of lavender as she passed him to sit at the opposite end of the table.

"I hope you don't mind if I sit here. I put Emily down for a nap so I'd like to try and catch up on some work," she said, placing her bag on the table.

"Not at all," he said and looked back at his computer screen.

"She downed that bottle super fast," she said with a laugh. "She's always ravenous after a bath." He gave her a polite nod. He was not going to engage her in a discussion about babies. He concentrated on the spreadsheet on his computer screen, pleased that she finally took the hint that he didn't want to talk anymore.

Ten minutes later he tried to ignore the humming coming from across the table. Sounded something like jingle bells, slightly more than off-tune. He looked up with an exaggerated sigh. She didn't get the hint as she started tapping her foot in time with her humming. She highlighted something from a book.

"What are you working on?"

She looked up from her book, obviously startled. "Oh, I'm studying."

He frowned. "For what?"

She bent her head again. "My PhD."

"PhD?"

She nodded.

"In social work?"

"No. Psychology." She took a sip of coffee then bent her head back in her book. He stared at the top of her head as she resumed her Christmas humming. He tried not to be impressed by her, but dammit, the more he learned about this woman the more he was intrigued by her and attracted to her. It was damn inconvenient.

"Why are you getting a degree in psychology?"

"Well, next year when I save enough money, I'd like to

finish my degree and then ultimately I'd like to be a child psychologist."

He didn't say a thing as he stared at the gorgeous woman across the table. *Run, Jackson, run far away.* She was beautiful, sweet, and smart. It was a hell of a combination. The women he dated were not nearly as dangerous as Hannah.

"Do you have any Christmas CDs?" Hannah stared at him from across the table, seemingly oblivious to his thoughts.

"Christmas?" Her preoccupation with all things Christmas wasn't the least bit attractive.

He rolled his eyes at her theatrical intake of breath, her hand flying to her chest. He refused to glance down at her chest again, knowing exactly where those thoughts would lead.

"Not even one?"

He smiled smugly. "Nope."

"I should have known," she said into her mug before she took a sip.

"Really? What gave it away?" He enjoyed talking to her way too much. For the first time in a long, long time, he felt like enjoying someone's company and not doing work. For the last ten years, he'd lived and breathed his company. He went to bed at night, sometimes with a woman by his side, sometimes alone, but always with work on his mind. When he wasn't working he thought about work. He hated holidays because it meant business couldn't be done. Work had been his salvation. Work was everything. But right now he could allow himself a brief respite with a beautiful, intriguing woman, couldn't he?

"I knew last night that anyone who didn't have a single decoration up must be a miserable, Ebenezer Scrooge type of person," she said jabbing her highlighter in the air at his direction.

A choked laugh escaped his lips. "Really, so because I don't have decorations you've come to the conclusion that I'm miserable and like Scrooge?"

She raised her eyebrows and folded her arms across her chest. "Then your subsequent behavior confirmed my hypothesis."

"*That again.* I already explained my behavior."

"Nothing you can say can excuse that behavior, Jackson. But not to worry, I understand that there are people in the world who are untouched by the spirit of Christmas—"

"Do you get commission from Santa Claus?" Jackson felt a smile spread across his face as she frowned at him.

"It happens to be my favorite holiday, that's all."

"Hannah, Christmas, as it exists in North America, is a commercially driven holiday. We're told we need to spend hundreds or thousands of dollars on loved ones in order to show we care. People tack on thousands in consumer debt and justify it by saying they have to for Christmas. I mean look at you, you're equating Christmas with something you need to *buy*—like a CD—with having Christmas spirit." He figured his high-handed tone was not at all appreciated when her frown turned into a glare. She didn't answer as she looked down into her book. He was surprised by the disappointment he felt when she didn't engage him anymore. He pretended to focus on the spreadsheet that didn't interest him at all.

Hannah's voice interrupted the silence a few seconds later and he ignored the surge of happiness he felt.

"Would you mind if I had a look at your stereo?"

He raised his eyebrows. "Be my guest."

She rose and walked over to the entertainment center. He let his eyes wander over her very enticing figure in the form fitting jeans she wore. If she could ease up on the holiday stuff and not mention his family again, they might even make it out of here tomorrow without an argument.

A moment later the sound of Bing Crosby's cheerful voice permeated the room, and *White Christmas* filled the cabin. Hannah sat across from him. Her green eyes sparkled and her smile was infectious. "Public broadcasting," she said smugly, picking up her BlackBerry.

He threw back his head and laughed.

She had put on small tortoise-shell rimmed glasses. He found them inexplicably attractive. "I tried it a few times and can't get a signal," she said, scrolling with her thumb.

"Yeah, mine's gone too."

She looked up at him, worry all over her face. "Is your land line working?"

He shook his head. "Gone when I woke up."

She bit on her lower lip, but nodded.

"I might have to get some firewood from the shed in case the power goes out for a while."

"Does that usually happen?"

"It's pretty typical for around here, but the power usually comes on within a day or so. I have more than enough wood in case that happens." He wanted her to feel safe and he didn't care to analyze why that was suddenly so important.

He was rewarded by a relieved smile tossed his way before she ducked her head back into her book. He didn't want the conversation to end.

"So what made you go into social work?"

She didn't answer him right away, almost as though she was carefully choosing her words before she looked up. "I knew I wanted to go into a profession that would help children, mostly because children can't help themselves. We live in a crazy world and they need someone to defend them and make sure they're safe."

Jackson swallowed hard as she stared him directly in the

eye across the table. "Must be hard work."

"If I can make a difference in someone's life, then it's worth it."

"So why do you want to leave?"

She took a deep breath. "I chose this career for the kids. I hadn't counted on the bureaucracy, the constant red tape that is always holding me back from doing what I think needs to be done."

"So I'm guessing you coming up here and tracking down a man who changed his name and trying to force me to adopt my niece isn't exactly the way things are done down at the child services bureau?" He didn't mean for that bite to enter his voice, and he obviously wasn't the only one who heard it. A flush, one that he found attractive even though he knew it was there because she was insulted, infused her face.

"I'd do anything to help a child, *especially* a baby. Besides, I'm doing what I should—the baby's mother asked me to find you."

He knew when to back down from an irate woman, and right now Hannah looked like she was ready to jump across the table and hit him. And he also knew she wouldn't appreciate knowing how cute she looked when she was angry. He admired her passion, and couldn't help but wonder if it extended itself to the bedroom. *Okay*...it looked like he was going to be battling that thought all day.

He held up his hands in surrender. She settled back into her chair, her posture not quite so rigid. "I don't have anything to lose, no one except the kids depend on me, so I don't care what bridges I burn to get the job done."

There was something in that statement, uttered so matter-of-factly, that irked him. She made it sound like all she had was her job, that she had no one else. As much as he resented why she was here, he couldn't deny the fact that she impressed him. A woman like her shouldn't be alone. She should have more than just the kids she helped through her job, more than her career.

Her head was back in her book, and after a few minutes of staring at his darkened computer screen he figured it out. They were very alike. He didn't have anyone worth caring about, and his job, his company was everything to him. He wasn't willing to let anyone come between his work and him—including a baby. He clenched his teeth, because it started to sound wrong, this line of thinking. He scowled at his computer. Before she crashed his escape-Christmas bash his world had been easy. Black and white. Now all this damn color trickled through. And Hannah. He didn't want to like her. He didn't want her to intrigue him.

• • •

Hannah tore the zipper of her purse open, acutely aware that Jackson wandered around the room. She wasn't going to get any studying done. So she looked for her favorite book to settle in front of the fire with. She looked up when she heard a rough sigh.

"What's this?"

"What's what?" She looked down to see that one of her books had fallen out of her bag and was now in Jackson's large, tanned hands.

She snatched it. Or tried to snatch it. "Let go."

He moved back a step, taking the book with him. She felt her cheeks ignite like a torch. He flipped it over and began to read the back blurb. The book was her favorite holiday read, but it was as personal to her as her past. Books had gotten her through many years of loneliness. They kept dreams alive inside her soul and taught her of love that always seemed so far from her reach. And until this moment she'd been glad it was with her. Ever since she could read, she was never without a book, especially at night, when all the disappointments haunted her mind as she tried to fall asleep. She'd huddle down under threadbare covers, in a room that never truly felt safe, and let herself be carried away to places where dreams actually came true. The words in her books would drown out the endless voices in whatever home she lived in. Her one drab red suitcase was filled with favorite books, each promising her an escape from her real life and she brought it with her to every home.

Seeing the book in Jackson's hand bothered her. It was too personal. She tugged at the book again. She thought she spotted the corner of his mouth twitch with a hint of a smile. She placed her hands on her hips and used her sternest voice. "Give me back the book."

He lifted his head. "Romance, huh? I wouldn't have you pegged as a romance reader."

She narrowed her eyes. "That happens to be one of my all-time favorite books, so if you'll excuse me." She grabbed the book from his hand. "I'd like to put it back in my bag."

He held up his hands and grinned boyishly, with an expression completely at odds with the angry, standoffish man that she was getting used to.

"It's nothing to be embarrassed about."

She frowned at him. The way he said it made it perfectly clear that he thought she should be very, *very* embarrassed. "You should probably read that book and take a few pointers on how to act with a woman." She couldn't believe she'd said that aloud.

He threw back his head and laughed.

She fought the urge to smile that gripped her out of nowhere. But it was tough, because his laugh was deep and a little throaty and a whole lot sexy. It transformed him.

He stopped laughing, but his smile remained, his perfect white teeth gleaming. "Really? So you think I'm lacking in the skills necessary to attract a woman?"

She crossed her arms in front of her. "Well, you *did* slam a door in my face."

He stopped smiling. "I did not *slam* it. I closed it."

"Twice. You slammed it twice," she said holding up two wiggling fingers.

He scowled at her and jammed his fists into his pockets.

"And then you yelled in my face, using your height and... er... *largeness* to intimidate me."

"I was not trying to intimidate you."

"And left me out in a blizzard."

He rubbed the back of his neck and then looked up at the ceiling. She could swear he counted to ten silently. "I came after you."

"And then let me fall because you *had* to hold the windshield scraper."

His eyes narrowed and his jaw clenched and unclenched. "I was not trying to hold the scraper, I was trying to convince you to come inside."

"And ruined all my Christmas cookies."

"I helped you pick them up. I had no idea there were cookies in that tin."

"Whatever, Jackson, you definitely don't know how to treat a lady." She grabbed her bag and dropped the book back in. There was a power and energy that emanated from him that was impossible to ignore.

"Hannah, if you weren't connected to my family, there would be no doubt in your mind that I know how to treat a lady."

She knew her neck and face were red. Jackson was

obviously the type of man who would have no trouble attracting women, but hearing the words come out of his mouth made it sound delicious, decadent.

"Nice line." She kept yanking at the zipper of her bag, wishing it would close.

She ignored him and what sounded like a muffled laugh. She needed to get this visit back on track. She needed him to be with Emily, to get him to slowly melt towards his adorable niece. Somehow, in the next twenty-four hours, she needed to break down Jackson Pierce's seemingly impenetrable walls… *bells.* She heard bells. Hannah looked up at Jackson who was still staring at her.

"Did you hear that?"

He shook his head. "Hear what?"

"Bells!" Hannah squealed, as they jingled again.

"Bells?"

She nodded and ran passed him to the window. Hannah inhaled sharply as a sleigh driven by two horses pulled up in front of the house. And the driver of the sleigh, well…

"Jackson?" she whispered with disbelief over her shoulder. "I think Mr. and Mrs. Claus are here."

"You expect me to believe that Santa and his wife are trolling around my front yard?" he asked, joining her at the window.

"They aren't *trolling*"

"Oh, God," he whispered, his face going white as he stared through the glass. Finally she had gotten through to him! Hannah ran to the door, but he beat her to it and blocked it. Arms crossed and giant frown across that handsome face did nothing to sway her determination.

Hannah tapped her foot. "I'm letting them in."

"No, you're not."

"*Yes*, I am," she said, trying to push him to the side. All that hard muscle didn't budge an inch. He just let out an irritated sigh. She stepped back and glared at him. "You can't honestly deny them entry!"

"It's not Santa," Jackson groaned, rubbing his temples.

"Well, who is it?"

"It's my crazy neighbors from down the street," he said, his voice sounding strained as the jingling grew louder.

"The house with all the decorations?" Hannah asked, thinking of the little cottage she'd driven past last night. It had been lit and decorated with such care that Hannah had slowed her car for a second to admire the lights.

Jackson nodded, his face grim. "That's the one."

They both jumped at the exuberant knock.

Hannah smiled up at him.

Jackson closed his eyes and mumbled something under his breath, turning around to open the door. A gust of arctic wind and a blast of boisterous bells greeted them.

Chapter Six

Hannah poured the Sampsons a second cup of coffee, listening with delight to their tale about the time they rescued a squirrel in a blizzard. Jackson was sprawled on the couch next to her, his legs crossed at the ankles, looking bored out of his mind. He caught her eye and held up a finger to his temple, pretending to pull the imaginary trigger with his thumb. Hannah frowned disapprovingly at him. How could he not like this couple?

"Oh, Hannah, what a delight you are, my dear. We've been cooped up for days with no one to speak to! We always worry about Jackson when he comes up to this cabin," Mrs. Sampson said, tsking at Jackson. "It's not healthy to be alone during the holidays. Do you know," Mrs. Sampson said, dropping her voice to a feverish whisper and leaning forward, "it's one of the most difficult times of year for many people?"

"I can't imagine why," Jackson's deep voice drawled. Hannah tried not to spill the contents of her mug of coffee.

The elderly woman nodded, her curly white hair bouncing in time, completely oblivious to Jackson's sarcasm. "Loneliness, dear. And that is why we came around to check on you. There have been so many times we've come over here looking for you, and in the distance we think we see lights on, but then when we get closer the house is always dark. It's a shame we always miss you!"

Hannah gasped and frowned at Jackson who shrugged slightly. How could he actually pretend he wasn't home?

"That is a shame, Mrs. Sampson. I suggest next time you try knocking harder. Jackson is a little hard of hearing I noticed. Sometimes, I think he's heard what I've said, but in fact he hasn't heard a word!" Hannah said, ignoring Jackson's loud coughing.

"I can assure you there's nothing wrong with my hearing," Jackson said, his mouth twitching slightly at the corner.

"Well, that's good. Looks like this little lady is worried about you though," Mr. Sampson said with a wink. "I can tell she's got a heart of gold, just like my Harriet." Hannah looked into her mug of coffee. She raised her head to clarify their relationship, but Jackson spoke first.

"She does have a heart of gold, Harry. She even baked a bunch of Christmas cookies and drove through a blizzard to see me." Hannah could hear the smile in his voice as he played along with this charade. She ignored the warmth that spread through her body from his words, knowing he didn't mean them.

Emily's soft cry interrupted her reply.

"Is that a baby?" Mrs. Sampson gasped, sitting up straight.

"No," Jackson snapped.

"Oh my, Jackson. You really do need to get your hearing checked, it is most definitely a baby!" Mrs. Sampson said, rising as Emily's cries continued. Mrs. Sampson looked as though she was going to explode if the baby's cries weren't answered. Hannah was trying to contain her smile as she crossed the great room.

"I'll make sure he gets a specialist to check him out, Mrs. Sampson. And I'll be right back, there is someone very important I'd like you to meet," she said, saying a silent prayer of thanks. This was exactly what she needed. Hannah tried not to skip down the hall on the way to her room.

She returned moments later to find Mrs. Sampson waiting at the end of the corridor, wringing her hands. "Mrs. Sampson, I'd like you to meet Emily." Mrs. Sampson rushed over to her side.

"Oh, she's precious, just precious! May I hold her, Hannah?" the woman asked with such joy in her eyes. "Look Harry, she's so little." Mrs. Sampson walked slowly into the great room and sat down next to her husband, as though she were holding the most fragile piece of crystal.

"She's a real cutie," Mr. Sampson said, touching a little tuft of Emily's hair. "A little angel," he whispered.

"Yes, an angel," Mrs. Sampson said, nodding.

Hannah stole a quick glance at Jackson. His calm, laughing demeanor was gone and she could see the tension in his body. He was standing in front of the hearth now, fire poker in his hand as he nudged some logs around.

"We had no idea that you two had a child," Mrs. Sampson whispered as Emily stared wide-eyed at her.

"Well," Hannah said, folding her hands together, "she's not really ours."

"She's my sister's child," Jackson said, his voice thick and stilted. "My sister died and this is her baby." Hannah tried to hide her shock that he would say anything to the Sampson's about Louise or Emily. He was trying. He was trying to be honest and her heart swelled with sympathy at the lines around his mouth.

"Oh, Jackson, we're so sorry," Mr. Sampson said, rising and patting Jackson on the arm. Jackson's expression softened as the much slighter, older man showed such compassion.

"Thank you," Jackson said with a terse nod.

"What about her father?" Mrs. Sampson said, her voice heavy with unshod tears.

"No father," Jackson said with a frown.

Hannah's body tensed. These people were here for a reason and she was going to use this opportunity to her full advantage.

"I want Jackson to be her father," Hannah said softly, though her voice sounded loud to her ears. She stared straight into Jackson's eyes, the silent challenge not evoking a response from him at all. He didn't look surprised by her statement, his mouth set in a grim line.

"What an honor that must be. She is a precious gift. There is nothing more special than a baby. Nothing on earth," Mrs. Sampson said, her eyes filled with tears as she looked from Jackson to Emily. Hannah's eyes didn't leave his face. His jaw clenched and he gave the woman a short nod. Hannah noticed he wouldn't look at Emily.

"Do you have children of your own?" Hannah asked, looking away from Jackson's intense stare.

Mrs. Sampson continued to rub Emily's back and a soft smile pulled at the corners of her mouth, the lines on her face deepening as she whispered, "We always wanted children. Always. But, well, Harry and I just weren't blessed in that way."

Hannah's heart ached as Harry ambled over to his wife, his own faded blue eyes shiny. She glanced over at Jackson, whose back had been to them, his shoulders rigid. She felt her own ache. What she would have given to have parents like the Sampsons. Their love was so real, their actions so pure.

"But we were blessed to have found each other," Mr. Sampson said brightly. His wife looked at him, nodding. She stood slowly and handed Emily over to Hannah.

"I think we've intruded on your time together long enough," Mrs. Sampson said, as Harry slipped his Santa hat over his head. Hannah followed them to the door as Jackson retrieved their red coats.

"It's been so nice to meet you," Hannah said with a smile as she stroked the back of Emily's head.

"Uh, yeah. Thanks for stopping by," Jackson said gruffly, standing next to her after he'd helped Mrs. Sampson into her coat.

"Are you sure you'll be all right getting back in this weather?" Hannah asked, as she glanced out at the blowing snow in the window. She ignored Jackson's nudge.

"Oh we'll be fine, I've been driving around in worse storms than this!" Mr. Sampson said, slapping Jackson on the shoulder. Jackson shook his hand and Hannah could have sworn she saw him smile. But when Mrs. Sampson leaned up on her tiptoes to give Jackson a kiss, his facade cracked and he gave the woman a smile that had her blushing and beaming. Moments later, as they were waving goodbye to the Sampsons, Hannah wondered if this visit had done it. Maybe it was that added piece of wisdom and insight that would compel Jackson to rise up.

"That was a fun night, don't you think?" Hannah said brightly, walking with Emily toward the kitchen to heat up a bottle.

"I'd rather dress up as a Santa in a shopping mall and have obnoxious kids sit on my lap. Good night."

Hannah stood in the doorway of the kitchen, baby bottle in one hand, Emily in the other, as she watched Jackson walk down the hallway. She was torn between chucking the bottle in the direction of his retreating figure and crying like a baby.

• • •

Jackson was done for. Seriously, cooked.

They were on day two of this horrid forced arrangement. After an evening straight from Hell thanks to the neighbors he'd managed to avoid for the last five years, he had woken up to the gorgeous sound of Hannah's laughter, which put him in an even fouler mood.

He'd trudged over to the window only to find the snow hadn't let up at all. It was the worst storm he'd seen in at least ten years. And for a guy that had gotten used to not feeling, he had spent the entire two days on some sort of roller-coaster ride of emotions. His biggest problem was that he began to *not* hate being cooped up in this cabin with Hannah and the baby. Hannah and his, er, *the* baby puttered around the house making all sorts of noises and happy baby-type sounds. Everywhere he looked Hannah was about. Cooking, singing to the baby, playing with the baby, changing the baby. And she was so damned loud that he'd been forced on more than a few occasions to glance over at them. When he did, he got an odd feeling in his chest when he saw that baby girl gurgling and staring at Hannah. And then he got some other, very inconvenient feelings when he looked at Hannah. Her smile, her hair, the sound of her voice—it drove him to distraction. He didn't get a speck of work done thanks to Hannah. He ended up losing game after game of solitaire on his computer while pretending to work.

And now that the baby slept it was the two of them in the great room again. The scene was annoyingly perfect. A storm blustered away outside while they were warm and toasty in his cabin. Even the constant Christmas songs were becoming less irritating. He was with a woman he found irresistibly sexy, who was also funny as hell, and smarter than anyone he'd ever slept with or contemplated sleeping with. But he couldn't even consider being with her because of who she was.

"Do you play cards?"

Jackson just stared at her. Had she said something?

"Hello-ooo? Earth to Jackson." Clearly exasperated with him she rolled her eyes. "I *said*, do you want to play a game of cards?" How was it possible a woman this intelligent could be this oblivious to the one thing they could be doing tonight? *Cards?* The last thing he felt like doing in a secluded cabin with a sexy, intriguing, and utterly beautiful woman was playing cards.

"Cards?" he spat out finally.

His derision did nothing to hamper her enthusiasm. "Yes, cards! Maybe we could have a game of crazy eights?"

"Crazy eights?"

She frowned at him. "Stop repeating everything I'm saying like all my suggestions are imbecilic."

"What the hell is crazy eights? That must be a game only small-town people play," he said, purposely baiting her.

She crossed her arms. "How do you know I'm from a small town?"

"Honey, you've got small town written all over you." His grin widened as her frown deepened.

"Oh really?"

"The books, the grandma hat, and bag—"

"Grandma hat! I'll have you know that a nice—"

He made a sweeping gesture with his hand, trying not to laugh. "A grandmother."

She stopped talking for a moment and tossed her hair over her shoulder. "Well, yes she is *a* grandmother. Just not my grandmother. Whatever. It may be a small town, but it's still close to civilization. Hope's Crossing is a charming—"

"*Hope's Crossing?* What kind of a name is that?"

She narrowed her eyes to slits and gave him a death glare. "It's a town filled with good old fashioned values, and people who care about each other. Everyone knows everyone—"

"Ugh, that sounds awful."

"But for your information, I grew up in the city."

"Really?"

She nodded but looked as though she was ready to shut down that conversation. He realized that whenever she told him something about herself, she seemed to regret it. He wasn't going to let her off that easy. "Why'd you leave?"

"I like small towns," she said, crossing her legs and not looking at him.

"I hate them."

"Of course someone like you would."

"Someone like me?"

She held out her hand and began rattling off a list on her fingers. "Closed-off, antisocial, miserly—"

"Miserly?" he said, laughing.

"I think we need to get back to deciding what game of cards we're going to play."

"I like hearing about you," he said, knowing she didn't want to tell him anything more about herself.

She turned her nose and then leaned forward in her chair, unrelenting. "I know what game we can play. How about asshole? Surely *you* must be very familiar with asshole"

He'd never known any woman to openly insult him as much as Hannah. And he liked the sound of her laughter when she joined in with him, and the way it lit up her face and gave him a glimpse of the woman she was when she wasn't afraid or worried. She was intoxicating. That realization made him stop laughing. "I'm not familiar with that game," he drawled out, and stood up. He walked over to the liquor cabinet. "Do you want a drink?" He certainly needed one.

"What are you having?" She stared at him with a sparkle and a lofty smile.

"Scotch."

"I'll have the same." He gave a half laugh, half grunt. Since when did he do a half-laugh? With Hannah he was constantly on the verge of laughing or yelling. She was full of contradictions.

"Maybe we should have the Sampsons over," Hannah said with a suspiciously cheerful grin.

He rolled his eyes. "I think once this season is enough."

"You're horrible. I can't believe you pretend you're not home when they knock at your door." She looked adorable as she tried to give him a stern frown even though her eyes twinkled.

"If I let them in once, that would be it. I'd never get rid of them," he said, walking back to her. He didn't want to think about all the things the Sampsons said about Emily being a gift. An angel.

"I think they're charming, and so in love after so many years. What wonderful spirit to have matching Santa hats…"

"I've got to start drinking."

Hannah threw her head back and laughed.

"Now if we're drinking this straight, we've got to do something more interesting than playing cards," Jackson said standing in front of her.

She raised a brow and tipped her head in silent challenge.

Jackson handed Hannah her glass and the moment her fingers brushed against his he felt the heat and fire that he'd been experiencing whenever he made close contact with her. She raised her glass to his and he wondered if he imagined the faint tremor in her hand.

"Cheers," she said, her voice husky. Jackson took a sip and

sat beside her on the leather couch. He noticed she scooted a little further away—she definitely felt the attraction too.

"So how about a game of truth or dare?"

"That seems a little juvenile for you, Jackson."

He leaned back and watched her over the rim of his glass. "I'm really just a kid at heart." He smiled at her shout of laughter, her whiskey swishing precariously close to the rim of her glass. "Besides, once we get a few of these in us," he said holding up his drink, "the game gets really interesting." He couldn't stop his smile at the thought of the petite brunette trying to drink him under the table.

"I'll bet. Okay, I'm up for it. But I've got to warn you, I'm not a cheap drunk, I know how to hold my liquor. Besides, there's a baby in the other room—I have to be responsible."

"All right, let the game begin."

"I go first," she said, leaning forward to pat Charlie on head.

"Shoot," he said, forcing himself not to look at the cleavage peaking out when she leaned over to pat his dog. It was impressive cleavage too. Dammit.

"Truth or dare?" she asked wriggling her eyebrows.

He folded his arms across his chest. "Dare."

She frowned. "Really? Dare?"

"Hannah, you didn't actually think I'd say truth, did you?"

She looked thoroughly disappointed. "No one ever picks dare!"

"Seriously? I always pick dare."

"But I haven't thought of a dare," she said, taking a long drink. She licked the corner of her mouth and his stomach clenched involuntarily.

"Time's a tickin'," he said, enjoying teasing her.

"No, it's not. There's no time limit. Okay, I've thought of something!" she said, looking very pleased with herself. "I *dare* you to tell me why you changed your name."

He laughed. "Nice work-around, but are you sure you want to waste a dare on something as mundane as my name?"

"Somehow I don't think this is going to be mundane at all." She lifted her eyebrows in silent challenge.

He groaned theatrically and then leaned further into the cushions. "Fine. When I…" He paused for a second searching for the right words. He'd never had to explain this before, and suddenly, not looking like a complete jerk to Hannah seemed important. "I knew that if I was ever going to make it I would have to disassociate myself from my family. I didn't want to be contacted by them anymore. I needed to move on with my life. I didn't do it out of embarrassment or shame. I don't really give a damn what people think of me." He finished off his glass and didn't look at her. Hannah was dangerously easy to talk to.

"I can understand that." The lack of sympathy in her voice startled him and he looked over at her. She shoved her empty glass in front of his face. "I'd love a refill, please."

"You and me both." He stood up and walked across the room. He felt a little slighted that she hadn't seemed more compassionate.

"Jackson?"

"Yeah," he said over his shoulder.

"Just bring the whole bottle."

His shoulders shook with laughter and did as asked, joining her on the couch. She surprised him by lifting her glass for a toast.

"To screwed up childhoods and bad Christmases," she said. He clinked his glass with hers and held her gaze.

"Really, bad Christmases? Screwed up childhood?" That wasn't what he expected at all from her.

She nodded. It was the first time she'd volunteered

anything about her life.

"I had horrible Christmases," she said, looking into her glass then up at him again.

"Then why do you love it so much?"

She smiled wryly. "I'm an eternal optimist, Jackson. I can't let my past dictate my future. I refuse to believe that it's an indicator of what I'm entitled to. I'm holding out for something better. I'm holding out for the best. I know that one Christmas I'm going to have everything I ever wanted. All the things that can't be giftwrapped, the important things…" Her voice caught at the end and he felt his own stomach twist at what she said. How the hell could they both have these similarities and yet be polar opposites?

She fidgeted with her glass. He guessed she felt a little awkward about what she'd said. "So you're waiting for some prince charming to come along and sweep you off your feet?" He winced inwardly at the callousness of his tone. It wasn't intentional, but it irked him that she thought that this perfect guy was going to come along and make her world.

"Oh, please. I'm not naïve, Jackson. I've seen a lot of horrible, truly sickening things. I'm not waiting for a man to make me happy."

"So what is it you want then? A family?"

She shook her head. "No."

That was not the answer he expected. She didn't want a spouse, a child?

"Why not?"

She shrugged. "I have a hard time with trust."

"With men?"

She held his stare for another second and then gave a sharp nod, her hair falling over her right shoulder. If she had been anyone else, he would have reached out to touch it, to see if it was as soft as the skin he felt the other night beside him in bed.

"Who hurt you?"

"I thought we were supposed to be playing a game here," she said, barely above a whisper.

"We are. And it's my turn."

She downed the rest of her drink, then turned to him. "No one."

"Bull. You nearly panicked when I touched you that night."

"I don't like being manhandled."

"It was more than that. You were totally freaked, like someone who's been—"

"Refill please."

He shook his head. "No way. I gave you a whole, long, honest answer. You're not getting away with that."

"Fine. I haven't exactly had a Cleaver style upbringing either. Let's say that I've had my share of run-ins with the wrong type of guy."

He felt his heart slam into his rib cage. He watched her expression closely as she turned her head and stared into the fire. "What happened?"

"That's two questions, Jackson." She was so quiet he had to lean forward to hear.

The thought of Hannah being brutalized by a man hurt him. It made him angry, made his gut twist and clench, and he was vaguely aware that his emotions were much stronger than they should be for a person he barely knew.

She tucked a wayward strand of hair behind her ear and lifted eyes that were filled with secrets and pain to his. He knew what it was like to be so private, how hard it was to share that past and that hurt with someone.

She smiled, and her expression completely changed. She had a gorgeous smile, the kind that made you want to smile back at her. But there was a part of him that was disappointed, because he really did want to know about her.

"My turn!"

But instead of asking him a question she jumped up and walked over to the table. His eyes didn't leave her as she came back with a plate of Christmas cookies she had baked earlier. He had a difficult time concentrating on what she was chattering on about while he was thinking about how nicely her jeans fit. She spun around at the exact moment his eyes had been admiring her behind. She lifted one arched brow and perched one hand on her hip. He grinned unabashedly.

"Did you hear a word of what I said?" she asked in a voice that made him think she could have been an excellent schoolteacher.

"I heard everything," he said lying.

"Then what did I just say?" He made the mistake of glancing down at her breasts, which were straining against her shirt. He couldn't help but think how nicely they'd fill his hands and then some…

"Jackson Pierce." He couldn't help it. He ducked his head and laughed, rubbing the back of his neck.

"Hannah," he said into her sparkling eyes, unable to stop the grin that seemed to appear on his face whenever he was around her. "I'm sorry, but you've got to cut me some slack. You are a beautiful woman."

She took a step closer and poked him in the chest and he resisted the urge to laugh. Something else hit him while he stared at her fiery eyes. When he first met her there was no way she would have poked him, but she trusted him now. She acted like her true, spunky, assertive self, and that made him feel damn good.

"Please save your lines for someone who'll actually fall for them," she said dryly.

He nodded. "Fine. Why don't you ask me what you're really dying to know?"

"And what would that be?" He could tell she was curious, and he didn't know if it was the whiskey or that his willpower had melted away after two days with this woman, but he was done denying his attraction.

"What it's like to kiss me."

Chapter Seven

What did he just say?

She quickly averted her eyes from his sparkling brown ones. She needed to act cool and flippant. "Absolutely *not* at all what I was thinking."

"But wanting?" He leaned towards her.

Her toes curled as she inhaled the smell of his aftershave. How could a man smell that good at the end of the day? "Wanting?" Jackson Pierce definitely knew how to charm a woman.

"You want me to kiss you." He hadn't stopped smiling and she couldn't either.

"I think you've had too much to drink." Hannah laughed.

"Hannah, two whiskeys wouldn't even alter my blood alcohol level," he said dryly.

She liked teasing him. It was electrifying and exciting, and it seemed so natural. If circumstances had been different and they weren't who they were, maybe this is what they could have been like. Now that they weren't talking about their pasts anymore she could relax. Or should have been able to if Jackson hadn't started talking about kissing her. The thought of her lips touching Jackson's was enough to send her running because she knew it would be sinfully good.

"Now you, on the other hand, you don't look like you can handle much more," he said smugly and poured himself another round. Hannah watched him swallow the liquid in one fluid motion, admiring how the muscles in his tanned neck flexed. He was too handsome for his own good. The sparkle in his eye told her that he knew she was checking him out, and liking what she saw.

She pursed her lips and used her most authoritative tone. "Actually, Jackson, I know exactly how much I can handle. I can drink four and a half shots of whiskey before I start acting like a moron. So fill'er up, buddy."

"Yes ma'am," he said with a laugh. "But now I want to know how you figured out that you can drink precisely that amount," he said, handing her a refill. When their fingers met, they both lingered for a few extra moments. She hoped her old calculation was still accurate. She was surprised she actually revealed that, because of course Jackson would want to know.

"When I was in college I thought it would be a wise endeavor to drink in the privacy of my room until I got royally wasted. That way I wouldn't have to worry about over-drinking when I went out with friends. So I finally got the amount right, and discovered that four and a half was enough without losing my head." She tried to sound matter-of-fact, and leave out any connotation that there would ever be any other reason than that. She finished with taking a long drink of her scotch. Jackson watched her pensively.

His brow furrowed. "So, let me get this straight. You sat in your dorm room by yourself and measured what your maximum dose of alcohol would be. Don't you think that's a little odd?"

She shook her head. "I don't like feeling out of control."

"I can understand that," he said with a nod. But she could tell that he knew there was more to the story. A part of her wanted to tell him everything. "A nineteen-year-old doesn't do that kind of thing."

"Well, this one did," Hannah said and held up her glass. "Now, if you don't mind I'll have that next shot. And I believe we were playing a game of truth or dare."

"You've been alone for a long time, haven't you?"

Hannah swallowed hard. Why would he ask that? It was the grandma hat. The books. Her holiday bag. He was learning too much about her. It was disconcerting. His feet were propped up on the ottoman in front of the sofa and he stared at the fire straight ahead, almost like he knew that if he looked at her it would be too personal. When she didn't answer right away he turned.

Hannah made the mistake of looking at his lips. He really shouldn't have such nice lips. They should have been thin, not sensual. He shouldn't have sensual lips. But her feelings went beyond how he looked. She shouldn't have enjoyed his company as much as she had today. Conversation with him was interesting and exciting. Being in such close proximity to him was unbearable because she wanted more from him, and that itself was a shocker. She had never wanted another man like him. She had never felt desire like this. The need for him to touch her, hold her, was so powerful that it made her want to ignore all the reasons she couldn't possibly ever pursue anything with him.

His question. She nodded finally, clearing her throat and looking away from him and the feelings he conjured up. "Yes, I guess I have been alone for a long time."

"Do you ever want to let go? Let someone take care of you?" His voice was gruff and sent shivers of pleasure throughout her body. She could hear the emotion behind his words, and the oh-so-tempting idea of letting someone take care of her, someone like him. But she knew what happened when you let your walls down and cared about people. There was always a reason someone couldn't love her enough to let her stay. It was a hard lesson she didn't want Emily to have to learn. *Emily.* She had nearly forgotten about Emily and why she was here. She hadn't broached the subject of adoption at all today, hoping that maybe if she lay off the topic he'd bring it up. But he hadn't. How could she be attracted to someone who refused to help his own flesh and blood? She finished her whiskey and turned to look at him. He still watched her with that I'm-going-to-kiss-you look that she had now identified. *Focus, Hannah.*

"What's really holding you back from adopting your niece?" she blurted out. She held her breath, because suddenly all the air seemed to have left the room. And the man that had been staring at her like he was about to make love to her mouth now looked as though he was ready to storm out of the room.

Just when she thought he was going to tell her to go to hell, his features turned calm. Eerily calm. "You did that on purpose, didn't you?" His words came out softly, but were laced with disappointment and accusation.

She felt her heart skip. "What do you mean?"

"We were having a nice time and you got scared. You brought up Louise's daughter to turn the conversation away from you and to kill any desire between us." She knew her face burned brightly, but she didn't answer him. He was only partially right.

"You don't want your niece to suffer because of Louise's mistakes."

"Louise knew what she was doing. I'm not going to pick up her mess anymore."

"A baby is not a mess," she said, her voice shaking with anger.

"Back off, Hannah," he said, walking away from her to stand in front of the fire.

"It's going to hurt you more in the long run, Jackson," she said speaking to his back.

"Somehow I doubt that."

"It will eat away at you. You are not the person you pretend to be. You are warm and you know how to love. I feel it, I sense it."

"Don't mistake desire for a beautiful woman for warmth and love," he snapped, turning to look at her. "Hannah, you have this naive, idealistic idea of who I am, but trust me, you're wrong. Not everyone is capable of being perfect like you, of doing the right thing."

She crossed her arms and looked at him accusingly. "Really? Then why didn't you let me drive home two nights ago?"

"I wasn't about to let a single woman drive those roads alone at night," he said with a shrug.

She smiled. "So you have a heart."

"Providing a stranger shelter from a storm and adopting a child are two entirely different things. Look, I even turn out the lights when an elderly couple comes looking for me. Not father material."

"Don't joke, and don't let your inability to forgive your sister prevent you from doing the right thing."

He turned his back to her again. The room was quiet, so still that it seemed surreal. The moon wasn't visible through the snow and wind. And neither were Jackson's thoughts.

"It looks like the storm will probably end sometime tomorrow morning," Jackson said, hands in his pockets, staring out the window. Hannah felt her stomach flip-flop as the reality of leaving set in. Things were more complicated now than before she arrived. She still hadn't convinced Jackson to even consider adopting Emily, and she had developed feelings for a man she should despise. Minutes passed as though Jackson had forgotten she was even in the room. Hannah toyed with the idea of having one more glass of whiskey, even though she knew that wouldn't solve anything. What she needed was divine intervention.

"Hannah, I admire your determination and your ability to fight for what you believe in. You're very convincing." His expression wasn't angry. He looked thoughtful and pensive.

Hope bloomed in Hannah's heart. Had she actually gotten through to him? Was this the miracle she'd been waiting for? "Really?" she whispered, meeting his gaze. She felt her palms turn sweaty as she waited for him to continue.

"What if I set up a trust fund for my niecc? She'll never have to worry about expenses or anything. It'll be more money than she'll need to live a wonderful life. She can even come and visit on holidays."

Hannah was unable to move for a minute. She processed what he said, wondering if there was some way she was misinterpreting. But there wasn't. She jumped up off the couch, her body trembling, her hands fisted at her sides. "What kind of cop-out, selfish, make-yourself-feel-like-a-hero kind of plan is that?" Through her rage she saw the genuine surprise on his face. "What, so she's going to come and see her rich uncle once a year and then go back to her foster home? Hey, you know if you register Emily as a charity, maybe you can claim all the money you give to her as a tax write-off too! I thought you were an intelligent man, but you're a selfish, uncaring idiot!" Hannah yelled, resisting the urge to pummel his chest with her fists.

"Let's get something straight," he said leaning down

so they were eye to eye. "I never claimed to be a saint. You came here, with your own naive expectations. What were you thinking? I'd just change my whole life for a baby I don't know? For a sister who didn't give a damn about her family?" He straightened up abruptly and then walked away from her, his long, angry stride taking him to the front door in an instant. She watched him shrug into his coat and didn't want him to have the last word, because his last words weren't good enough.

She followed him to the door. "Yes. Yes, that's exactly what I thought. Because if someone came to me and said that I had a niece that desperately needed me I would drop everything. I would rearrange my entire life if I found out I had family."

"Then you obviously don't know a damn thing about the kind of family I had," he said, zipping up his coat in one angry motion.

"Stop using your past as an excuse to be a jerk for the rest of your life!" She inched closer to him, not feeling the least bit intimidated as he stared down at her. "You could have your own family. You have the power to change everything, to do something really meaningful. She would be your *daughter*. If you had a little girl that looked up to you and thought you were the best daddy in the whole wide world, wouldn't you do everything for her, to keep her safe?" Hannah didn't give him a chance to answer before continuing.

"If I had a dad that came home to me every night and lifted me in his arms and kissed me, I'd know that I was loved, that I was wanted. If I was sad and thought the whole world was against me, but I had a daddy that loved me, and was there when I cried, or was there to pick me up when I fell, then I would know that everything was going to be okay. That's what every child should have, Jackson. If this were a perfect world, then every child would have enough food in their stomach, a warm bed at night, and a parent who would walk through fire to keep them safe. I don't care how important your career is to you or how your sister screwed you over or how many times your father hurt you. You are a grown man and you have the power to change your future and that baby's future. You're a coward if you turn your back on her. How can you go to sleep at night, not knowing where your niece is? Not knowing if someone is hurting her? How *dare* you refuse her!" Hannah didn't care that tears were streaming down her face when she finished. She didn't care that she'd just revealed her innermost yearnings as a child, she didn't care that she was visibly shaking.

He didn't answer and Hannah stood there, letting him see her cry, hoping that she'd gotten through to him. He stared at her for a few seconds, his eyes glittering, his cheek flexing.

"I'm going to get firewood, I need some fresh air." His words came out in a cold, clipped tone and he didn't make eye contact with her. He whipped open the front door and then turned to her, pausing at the threshold. "If Charlie needs to go outside, make sure you put him on a leash and don't go past the back deck."

She gave him a sarcastic salute with her hand while she shook with rage. He said something under his breath and walked out.

She forced herself to take a few deep breaths and collapsed onto the sofa. She needed to regain control, she thought, trying to catch her breath. He had ignored everything. She wasn't going to get through to him. Charlie came over to sit in front of her. She buried her face in his warm fur, gently stroking him. A few minutes later she forced herself to regain control. "Charlie, I'm not giving up just yet. I've got until tomorrow," she mumbled. Charlie laid a furry paw on her knee and whined.

"At least you understand," she said. He scratched at her leg and then trotted over to the back door and scratched it, turning to look at her. "Oh, I guess *that's* what you wanted," she said with a sigh, rising and grabbing her coat

She walked into the kitchen and pulled on her boots. She went through the motions of putting on her hat and mittens, though her mind was on Jackson. It was still blizzard-like conditions and she knew how dangerous it could be in case they got too far from the house. She opened the broom closet and found a yellow toolbox. She flipped open the lid and found a rope right away in the perfectly organized box.

"Figures he'd be this neat," she mumbled. She paused for a moment, then purposefully took a few screws and bolts out of their compartments and dropped them into other compartments. She felt a little better as she snapped the lid shut. After hooking Charlie's leash around his collar, she swung open the door, the cold blast making them both step back a second.

"Okay, boy, make this quick," she yelled above the wind. She squinted, trying to keep an eye on Charlie as he pulled at the leash. It was almost impossible to see even a foot in front of them. How was Jackson able to be out in this for so long? Charlie kept nudging her down the steps, refusing to do his business anywhere near the deck. "You're as stubborn as your owner, Charlie. Hold on, I'm going to tie this rope around the banister so we don't get lost." Charlie waited obediently while she tied a double knot around the wooden handrail.

Hannah tried to focus on not falling in the deep snow. She lost her grip on the leash and swore under her breath while Charlie ran off, exhilarated by his freedom. Hannah yelled after him, forgoing her hold on the rope, instinctively choosing to run after the dog. A few steps out into the almost waist-high snow, the porch light was now impossible to be seen through the thick wind. She yelled Charlie's name as loud as she could, careful to keep her bearings so she'd be able to walk back to the house. At the sound of a bark she spun around, but there was still no sign of Charlie. She ventured out a few more steps, knowing the situation was getting more and more dangerous. She didn't have her rope to guide her back and she knew how easily a person could become disoriented and lost in a blizzard. She turned around to where she thought the deck should be and began trudging through the snow, feeling the snow seep through her clothing.

Seconds turned into minutes and Hannah tried not to panic as the only sound she could hear was that of ice pellets, and the only thing she could feel was a frigid cold seep through her. She kept calling for Charlie but couldn't hear anything except her own voice engulfed by the wind. She trudged along, but with each step felt herself move farther and farther from any chance of finding Charlie. Or the cabin.

No one was going to find her out here. Even if Jackson looked for her, it was impossible to find a person in this. She needed to find her way back on her own. She had been in trouble before. She could do this. She could find her own way back—despite the fact that merely moving her legs through the snow was becoming more and more laborious. There was no way a blizzard was going to be her ending. Emily needed her.

Chapter Eight

Jackson piled the wood logs on the porch and stomped his feet, snow tumbling off his boots. He was used to winters like this, growing up in the North. He actually had a few fond memories of his dad, before his mother died. His father had been kind and patient. Jackson would follow him out to the barn and watch as he'd chop wood for the fire. As a kid, he didn't quite grasp how dangerous the weather was, though his father had drilled into him how deadly it could be.

Jackson stretched his arms wide, feeling better having worked off some of his frustrated energy while getting the firewood. He hadn't thought about anything other than Hannah and her accusations. He had never gone from desire to pure anger in a matter of minutes with anyone in his life. Hannah knew how to push all his buttons. She'd made his idea about giving his niece money sound like he was a villain. The more he thought about what she'd said the more he realized how she was right. She got to him. Everywhere.

The glow of the fireplace from the porch made him stop for a moment. For a second he could have sworn he smelled his mother's baking. And for a moment, he didn't know why, he let himself stay in the past. He remembered when he'd race into the house after school, his mother stopping him with a smile and shake of her hand, reminding him to take off his shoes. That feeling of love that was always there drifted through him. His little sister would worship him and tag along with him. When did it all go wrong? Why hadn't their father been stronger for them? He could see all their faces, smiling, laughing around the dinner table.

It had been years since he'd let himself think back to those days. Jackson cursed under his breath knowing his mother would be horrified if she knew he rejected his only niece, his only family because of his anger toward his sister. He rejected her grandchild. That didn't make him much better than his father, did it? He stamped his feet and fisted his hands so tightly they were painful. He knew what he had to do because no matter that he'd changed his name, he was still his mother's son and she had raised him better than this.

Jackson blinked back the moisture in his eyes that he knew must be from the ferocious wind, and not some overzealous emotions. He cleared his throat and mentally braced himself for his next encounter with Hannah.

He knew something was wrong the second he walked into the eerily quiet house. He strode down the hallway to Hannah's bedroom. His eyes narrowed in on Emily, who slept contentedly, but there was no Hannah anywhere. Then he heard the sound of paws scratching the back door and he strode across to the back room, not bothering to take off his wet boots or coat. Sure enough, Charlie was outside on the porch scratching at the door. A sick feeling gripped him as he opened the door and Charlie barked furiously at him. Charlie shook himself clear of snow and continued to bark. The porch light was on, Hannah's coat and boots were gone, and Charlie had been outside by himself.

He cursed and whipped open the back door, making sure Charlie stayed inside. Genuine fear for Hannah propelled him to act fast as he spotted a half-tied rope on the deck banister. There were no footsteps in sight, which didn't surprise him. Between the pace of the falling snow and the ferocity of the wind, it would be impossible to track someone in this. He secured the rope and ventured down the steps.

Jackson yelled her name over and over again, squinting against the harsh onslaught of snow. Adrenaline coursed through him as he continued to call out for her, his voice hoarse from the strength of his yell. He swung the floodlight in a circular motion, trying to catch a glimpse of motion. The yard immediately behind the house was free from trees, but he knew if she walked more than thirty feet, the forest would start and would be a deadly maze. If she went in there…he forced himself to stop thinking about how unlikely finding her would be as the minutes ticked by.

He circled the flashlight again and paused for a second, thinking he spotted a flash of color. He moved the light slowly, praying for the first time in his memory for help from above. And there it was. Red. Her pom-pom hat. He kept the light focused on the patch of red and moved as quickly as he could through the snow. He called her name over and over again and came in closer, until finally he could see her face. She screamed out his name and tried to move toward him.

It was the sweetest damn sound he ever heard.

He knew at that moment that Hannah Woods meant a hell of a lot more to him than he wanted to admit. The need to protect her overwhelmed and consumed him. He didn't question it, he didn't analyze the why. All he knew was that he needed her in his arms. He could tell from how slowly she moved that he'd arrived just in time. He swallowed up the remaining distance between them in a few strides. When she was right in front of him he saw how red her face was and the blue tinge to her lips.

"You okay?" He wrapped his arms around her and felt her hands clutch his coat.

She nodded against his chest, but he wasn't convinced. "Hold on, sweetheart," he whispered, the endearment coming naturally, though he'd never said it to anyone before. He leaned down and picked her up. Instead of protesting like he half expected, she just curled her face into his neck and wrapped her arms around him.

He let the rope guide them back to the house and prayed that she didn't have frostbite. He gently put her down on the porch, his arms grasping hers, making sure she was steady. "Come on," he said, opening the door and taking her hand to get into the house. He had experience with frostbite and cold weather exposure, but this was different, this was Hannah. Courageous, beautiful, smart Hannah. Standing a few inches from her in the darkened kitchen, she raised her green eyes to his and he was torn between wanting to kiss her and yell at her for taking such a crazy chance outside. But the look in her eyes took his breath away. He knew it wasn't just him that felt this crazy connection. He knew it in the softness, the complete candor in her eyes. She wasn't hiding from him anymore.

• • •

"What were you thinking?"

In spite of the pain she felt as the warm air pierced her cold body and the shaking consumed her, she heard the tenderness. She saw the worry in his handsome features, noticed the faint tremble in his strong, capable hands, and it warmed her in a way that nothing ever had. When she heard him calling her name through the blizzard she knew that everything was going to be okay. He'd called her sweetheart. No one had ever called her anything so wonderful. She trusted Jackson, and she had never trusted anyone before. But God, it had felt good to lean on someone, to trust someone with her life. Nuzzled in the reassuring strength of his body, she realized that he had put her ahead of his own safety. Jackson was the only person who had ever put her first.

"Emily?"

He nodded. "She's fine. Sleeping."

Hannah smiled shakily at Charlie, who sat and watched her. If there was ever a worried companion, it was him.

"You could have died if I hadn't found you."

Hannah's eyes filled with tears, her throat burning. She tried to move, but everything hurt. "I can't move my fingers yet," she said, holding her hands out in front of her. He gently reached out and enveloped her fingers in his hands. His touch reached that part of her that she had always wondered about, the part that had been shut off so many years before, the place the therapist told her would be there when the right person came along, if she let it happen. She stared at his fingers intertwined with hers, feeling the heat and the strength that radiated from his hands. Of all the people in the world, how could it be him? The one man she was ready to let in?

She didn't want to think about why he was wrong for her, because as much as she wanted to deny it, her feelings, her attraction, didn't care about why he was wrong. There had never been anyone so right. In twenty-eight years, she had never felt truly safe. Until tonight, when he found her in a blizzard and carried her so protectively—like she mattered, like she was important.

Jackson pressed her fingers against his face. She closed her eyes and shuddered, partly due to the pain, and partly because of the pleasure of feeling that strong jaw, the tickle of his stubble. She lifted her eyes to his, transfixed by the warmth, the fire in them. When he took her hands and kissed each palm, holding it to his lips, she felt her knees slowly start to give. She wanted to lean in to him, to give in to the overwhelming desire to be held and touched by him.

"Do you know how fast people can get lost out there?" he murmured against her hands, his breath hot and oh so delicious against her cold skin. She had a hard time concentrating, her mind distracted by the sight and feel of his lips.

"Obviously. And I knew what I was doing," she said, the chattering of her teeth abating. She tried to focus on the conversation and not on the sensation that his lips were causing. "I've seen the *Little House on the Prairie* episode where they get snowed in and they tie a rope from the house to the barn." The look he gave her almost made her laugh out loud. Almost.

"Hannah, do not tell me you are getting your advice on how to brave a blizzard from a stupid TV show."

She frowned at him, feigning insult. "It's not a stupid show. It happens to be my all time-favorite show."

"You could have *died*. Charlie is a *dog*." It sounded as though the words were ripped from his heart. Hannah felt every bone in her body melt and every speck of laughter that had teased her seconds ago was gone.

She shook her head. "I know what he is. I know what he means." Her voice sounded odd to her ears. Maybe it was the cold or maybe it was the emotion in her throat as she spoke. She didn't want him to feel alone anymore, didn't want him to think that no one else could understand. She knew why he was afraid of adopting his niece now. She had been wrong. He wasn't selfish, he was afraid. Jackson was a man that gave the people he loved everything. He gave them himself and the betrayal of disappointment, of abandonment was more painful than he could bear.

His eyes turned a deeper shade of brown, his voice a gruff whisper. "What do you mean?"

She swallowed hard. She couldn't back down, she couldn't be a wimp her whole life. She wanted to jump into the safety of his arms and stay there, start there. Become the woman she always dreamed of being but never wanted to. Until now. She looked into his eyes, embracing the warmth she saw staring back at her. "I know, Jackson, I know what it's like to feel that no one loves you, that you're not worth fighting for." Those last words were torn from some place deep inside her. And for all the therapy she'd ever had, nothing had ever healed like this. Hannah placed her hand on his jaw and a sensuous heat warmed her body. She didn't look away as the shock registered in his eyes. He covered her hand with his, staring at her.

Hannah took a step into him, close enough that if she leaned her head forward the solid, hot warmth of his chest could be under her cheek. She wanted to drink in his scent, his heat, his fire, and place her lips on the hot skin exposed at the collar of his shirt.

His hands framed her face and she tilted her head back to look at him. "I know your pain, *I know*—" She didn't know she was crying until she felt his lips swoop down and capture the wetness that poured from her eyes. He kissed and sipped, and branded her with sweet promise. His lips traveled her face and finally slipped lower until they touched hers.

They tasted and teased until she opened her mouth with a sigh. A voice, a sound that she didn't even know she could utter, escaped her throat as his tongue tangled with hers. She had been waiting for him forever. His tongue tasted, tormented, and made love with hers so that breathing was impossible. They fumbled with each others' buttons, hot fingers tangling together, their lips never parting. When the jackets fell to the floor in a heap, Jackson lifted her in his arms, carrying her to the couch and lowering her with a frenzied gentleness. She reached up for him and he covered her body with his. All that she let herself feel was the desire that ripped through her faster than a hurricane. She knew she needed to let him in, to trust him.

When his tanned hands went to lift her sweater she urgently helped him shrug it off. And any shyness she ever thought she'd have was snapped away by the desire she read in his eyes, and by her own need to take off his clothes. She tugged at the hem of his shirt, and he drew it over his head and tossed it to the ground, their eyes speaking the words that neither of them were able to say. She felt a throbbing heat escalate with each kiss that he placed on her exposed skin, and soon it felt like Jackson was everywhere.

She plunged her fingers into his soft hair as his head trailed the length of her torso, down to her stomach, and then back up until he reached her breasts. She arched her back when she felt his hands circle around to unclasp her bra. When she felt his mouth move from her earlobe and trace her collarbone with kisses she shivered. But when he found her breasts, his lips tasting and then suckling her nipple, she cried out. Hannah threaded her fingers through his thick hair, pressing his head against her breasts.

"God, you're so beautiful, more beautiful than I dreamed," he said before he moved his sweet torture to the other breast. She felt swollen, heady with an insistent sort of desire.

He was strong and powerful, but she felt no fear. Firelight made his tanned skin seem more touchable, more alluring. The reality of what she was doing started trickling into her mind, like a stream at the first thaw of spring, but there would be no spring with Jackson. There would be one night.

"Jackson," she whispered, his name sounding more like a moan as his lips tormented her skin.

"Mm-hmm," he answered, clearly not listening. She sucked in her breath as his tongue circled her nipple decadently.

"I can't do this."

"What do you mean?" he said, his head lifting. She couldn't quite make his expression.

She could feel the cold air send goose bumps over her bare skin, despite the blush that she knew began to engulf her as Jackson stared at her, bracing himself on his forearms.

"I mean, this," she said waving her hand between them, searching for some words to explain her sudden change of heart, something that could make him understand.

Her voice trailed off as he lifted himself off her slowly. She felt for her shirt with her hands, keeping her eyes glued to him. The most profound, intimate, unbelievable experience she'd ever had with anyone and she'd ruined it. Jackson exhaled raggedly and ran his hands down his face.

"I'm sorry," she said reaching out to touch him but stopping herself, not really knowing whether or not he'd pull away. Why couldn't she just let herself go? Let Jackson take her to that place of sweet oblivion? As she stared at his muscular back, her eyes wandering over what her hands had worshipped, she knew why. If she slept with him she would fall in love with him, and loving Jackson would be impossible. Loving anyone, giving anyone that kind of trust, that kind of power over her was inconceivable. She had spent her entire life trying to gain freedom and to give it up was unthinkable.

"I'm sorry," she whispered again as she stared at his back. As much as she was sure she'd made the only decision she could, this never should have gone this far. He reached a part of her no one ever had.

"I, I need a second."

"I feel really, really stupid right now," Hannah said, drawing her knees up to her chest and wishing the couch would swallow her whole. She wrapped her arms more tightly around herself, wishing she'd found her shirt. Jackson leaned down and picked up his shirt, then gently drew it over her head. She pulled her arms through, inhaling his scent, feeling the soft cotton envelop her like a blanket. The firelight cast a warm hue over his muscular physique, making him appear more powerful, more beautiful than she ever thought a man could be.

"You're okay?"

Hannah nodded, unable to speak past the cowardly lump in her throat. *Explain to him why. Tell him you want nothing more than to let go of the past and spend tonight in his arms… tell him you want him to be the first man to touch you and hold you and love you.* Hannah stared at Jackson, her thoughts screaming through her mind, but nothing came out of her mouth. Jackson's jaw clenched, almost as though he sensed her battle. But still she couldn't open her mouth.

"Goodnight then," he said and turned away slowly. He gave her more than enough time to call after him. More than enough time to admit she made a mistake.

• • •

Jackson stared at the ceiling. It had been an hour since he left Hannah in the living room. Right now he felt more like punching his fist through the window and braving the storm outside than trying figure out the woman across the hall from him. He was mad at himself for even giving in and allowing himself to touch her and kiss her. In just a few hours he'd gone from shaking with rage at her high-handed speech, to the humbling realization that she was correct, to gut-wrenching fear that she was lost in a blizzard, to inexplicable gratitude and relief when he found her, to the height of a desire that he'd never felt with anyone, to being completely left out in the cold. He'd thought there was some kind of connection that they were sharing more than a physical encounter. And then she'd ended it.

Jackson rubbed his eyes with the back of his palm. Sleep would be a futile endeavor tonight. A part of him wanted to ask her what was wrong. When they were in the kitchen she'd whispered that she knew what it was like to be alone, that she had always been alone. Why? Where was her family? He played back all of their conversations in his head and he couldn't remember one in which Hannah mentioned her family.

And then there was Emily, and the royal putdown he'd received when he told Hannah his plan. He could smile about it now. She was right. How could he willingly let his niece live in foster care when he was more than able to provide her with a home?

His thoughts ran back to their argument before he stormed out of the house. He remembered the exact look in her eyes, the anger in her face as she yelled at him. Jackson sat up in bed as the realization that Hannah had spoken about herself dawned on him. It all made sense. Her fear of him. Her career choice. And tonight's sudden withdrawal. He didn't know the details but his gut told him he was right, and for once he wished he wasn't. The urge to track down everyone who'd ever hurt her gripped him. He wanted to protect her. And he hadn't felt the need to protect anyone in a long, long time.

He was going to go face his past and future. He was going to try and reclaim a little of the person he had been when his mother was alive. He was going to be the uncle Emily needed him to be.

But he wasn't going to do it without Hannah.

Chapter Nine

Hannah hadn't felt this low in a long, long time. It was just like when she was a child, when she thought there was someone to save her, there would be a complication to ruin it, and it broke her heart to see the same happen to Emily.

She zipped up her bag as quietly as she could, not wanting to wake the baby yet. She'd get the car loaded up and then come back in for Emily. The less time either of them had to spend with Jackson this morning, the better. She had failed Em and she had failed Louise. Her instincts had been wrong about Jackson. She'd let her attraction for him cloud her judgment—she had never made so many mistakes at once.

Hannah walked down the hall, patting Charlie when he trotted over to her. She didn't want to see Jackson. She had no idea how she could look him in the eyes and be able to hide her disappointment. She wouldn't cry when he said goodbye to his niece today, to her. She'd wait until she was in the car, safely away from the cabin.

She walked into the great room, her heart and feet stopping. Jackson was standing next to the unlit hearth, his eyes on hers, his lips set in a narrow line. Her eyes went from his handsome face to the bag beside his feet. She stared at him, not daring to ask what she hoped more than anything in the world.

"I'm going to adopt her." His voice broke the silence in the room. His eyes held hers and everything inside her went still. She bit her lip, trying desperately to hold on to her emotions. She didn't want to believe, couldn't. His image turned blurry. Those were the words she'd prayed for as a child in foster care. They were the words that would have saved her. She had spared Emily and kept her promise to Louise. Relief and gratitude tore through her. Her bag slipped off her shoulder, falling to the ground with a thud. She tried desperately to find some air, but her breath came in shallow gasps…

Her chin fell to her chest, and she placed her hands over her eyes. Seconds later Jackson was there, with the tenderness he'd shown her last night, and gently moved her hands and folded her into his arms.

"I have absolutely no idea what I'm doing," he whispered against her hair.

"You don't have to," Hannah said, her face against his chest, the warmth she felt from Jackson so addictive.

"I hope you know what you're doing."

She nodded firmly. "I'll be there every step of the way during the adoption process. I'll help you in any way I can."

"I have your word?" he asked, leaning back to look at her, an odd light flickering across his eyes.

She'd do anything for Emily. "I promise. I'll do whatever it takes," Hannah said, smiling up at him.

• • •

Hannah opened the door to the dingy, stuffy government office that had been her second home for the last five years.

She had only been gone five days and yet she felt as though it had been months. She felt more confident, more determined… but more vulnerable. Her facade was cracking. She was letting people in.

But she had done it. She had convinced Jackson. He was in Hope's Crossing, ready to start the paperwork. Nothing could have prepared her for the moment he told her he was going to adopt Emily. She didn't know what prompted his change of heart and at that moment she didn't need to know.

They had dropped Emily off at Mrs. Ford's, who was ecstatic to hear that Jackson was going to adopt his niece. Hannah had asked Jackson to wait for her in the car while she dealt with work. The last thing she wanted was him witnessing what was sure to be a major reprimanding from Jean. First Hannah needed to get the situation under control and then she could invite Jackson in to get started on the paperwork.

"Welcome back," Hannah whispered under her breath as she stepped inside. Old metal desks, the kind that must have still been ugly when they were new in the sixties, the stale smell of old office building combined with burned coffee reminded Hannah that she really hadn't been away all that long. The small blinking Christmas tree in the front window, sadder than Charlie Brown's, hummed along with the rest of the electrical equipment that hadn't been updated.

Hannah made eye contact with Allison, who was on the phone. Her friend's eyes looked like they were ready to pop out of her pretty face as Hannah walked in. Allison pretended to slice her neck with her finger as Hannah approached, clearly warning her that Jean was royally ticked.

"Hannah. Nice of you to show up." Jean's thin face was pinched and her narrow eyes even beadier than usual as she marched towards Hannah. Nothing like a little office drama to lighten up the mood at the social services department.

Hannah thought she looked more and more like the wicked witch from the *Wizard of Oz*, except dressed for the twenty-first century, *kind of.*

"Hi, Jean," Hannah called out in her most chipper voice, smiling. Hannah refused to let her nerves take over. This was a victory, no matter what. No one was going to ruin this for her.

Jean came to an abrupt halt in front of her, steaming coffee in hand. The mug boasted the caption *World's Best Boss* in faded letters, and Hannah and Allison always joked that Jean had probably bought the cup for herself.

"Hannah, there's a box on your desk filled with all of your belongings. Take it, get out."

Hannah ignored her. "I found Emily's uncle. He's here. He's going to adopt her." Hannah felt her stomach begin to churn when Jean didn't react to her news. Jean stared at her like a dead fish.

"I don't care. You crossed the line. Pack your things. You no longer work for social services."

She'd known this would be a possibility, but she had thought that if she were able to find Jackson and have him agree to the adoption, Jean would see it as a victory. She had braced herself for probation or a reprimanding, but not firing. Hannah took a steadying breath. She tried to ignore Allison, who made stabbing gestures with her plastic bagel knife towards Jean. "You don't understand, Jean, he will be her legal guardian."

"I already have a placement for Emily lined up. You had no right running off to track down this man. This is the third time you've been in direct violation of office policy and you received a warning each time—"

"I had *every* right to track him down. Louise wanted him to be Emily's guardian. He is next of kin. You knew full well that I was going to do everything to find him. This isn't about me. It's about doing what's right. How are you going to deny next of kin adoption rights?"

"Let's make sure you're clear on where we stand," Jean said, setting her coffee cup down on an Allison's desk. "You have broken so many rules here I can't even remember. Even though you seem to a have a bunch of people willing to cover up your dirty work for you, I'm on to you. This is the final straw. You almost got yourself raped, you got beaten, and now you kidnap a baby. You're too much trouble. I have to file way too much paperwork on your behalf. You are done here."

Hannah felt her body shake with rage. Damn Jean and her black and white rules. She had always been able to separate the emotional aspect of her job. She never made any decision based on instinct, but then again, Jean hadn't stepped foot outside the office in years. Hannah took a deep breath as Jean handed her a file. A thick one. Hers.

Hannah ignored it.

"Jean, we are talking about a family member. You know that's different, you know that he would receive priority. He wouldn't have to jump through any hoops to adopt her," she said, trying to sound calm and logical, even though she was very tempted to pour that cup of coffee all over Jean's wiry body and see if she melted.

"There are steps and procedures that need to be followed." She shoved the file in her direction again. Hannah shoved it back.

"That you have the power to speed up and make happen. This isn't a favor. Louise was my case and she left me with her wish that Emily's uncle adopt her!"

Jean started a cackle that ended with a bad fit of smoker's cough. "She was probably high as a kite when she wrote that note, Hannah."

"Don't go there, Jean."

"Maybe if you had kept a closer eye on her—"

"Back off, lady."

Hannah almost jumped at the sound of Jackson's voice. She had no idea when he'd walked in. She turned around slowly, vaguely aware that everyone else in the office was watching. She also didn't miss Allison's surprised smile. Jackson's face had that hard look that she had seen before, but his eyes were colder than anything she'd witnessed from him. His back was straight and his eyes glittered with unmistakable anger. It felt strange to know that it was on her behalf. The most shocking thing, though, was that she wasn't annoyed that he spoke up to defend her, that he'd ignored her request and walked in here. She almost didn't even care that he heard what Jean had said. Was this what it was like to have someone guard your back?

"I don't answer to you, sir," Jean said stiffly.

"Well, you can be damn sure I'll find out who you do answer to. That baby is going home with me."

Hannah felt her anger dissipate. Jackson knew how to get what he wanted. The brown eyes that could be so warm now glittered with a hostility that was palpable and his hard jaw was set. Oh yeah, Jackson was royally pissed. He looked very out of place in the poorly furnished grey and metal office. Somehow, even dressed in jeans, the man exuded power and wealth.

"You go ahead, but when her permanent placement gets approved you'll be in for a rude awakening. Your sister's letter won't hold up in court and a single male is not exactly the best candidate for a family," Jean said smugly.

"You mean you haven't told her, Hannah?" Jackson asked smoothly, glancing down at her, a smile on his face that wasn't quite reflected in his eyes.

Hannah could have sworn she saw everyone lean forward in their chairs. The excitement radiating from her best friend as they made eye contact could have powered the entire office.

"I, uh." What was Jackson talking about? Hannah felt his hands wrap around her shoulders, pulling him to her side. What was he doing?

"Why don't you tell her about our marriage?" Jackson said, kissing the side of her neck. Hannah felt her knees jiggle and Jackson's grip on her tightened, as though he knew she was about to fall on her face.

"Marriage?" Jean said.

Jackson nodded.

Allison squealed, jumping up, her chair crashing into the wall.

Hannah surreptitiously dug her heel into Jackson's foot.

Chapter Ten

"So much for gratitude," Jackson grumbled, and limped outside.

"I *knew* you were mentally unbalanced!" Hannah hissed. The cold winter air felt good on her flaming cheeks as they stood facing each other on the sidewalk. Shoppers passed by them, the sound of Santa's ringing bell could be heard, but the only thing Hannah could focus on was the memory of Jackson telling Jean they were getting married tomorrow. He was totally nuts.

"Earth to Jackson Pierce!" She focused on him, trying to figure out his expression. He looked like he was ready to kill someone. Maybe the reality of what he proposed had sunk in, or maybe he really was upset about her letting Louise down.

"What the hell was that woman talking about?" The trademark jaw clenching was back so Hannah knew he was royally peeved about something.

"What? How about explaining what *you* were talking about?" Hannah glanced over each shoulder. In small towns there was always someone ready to eavesdrop on a conversation. He must have sensed her trepidation since he grabbed her hand and started walking towards his car. He walked so quickly that she had to run to keep up. Hannah jerked to a stop, yanking him to a halt with her. Jackson turned to glare at her.

He closed his eyes briefly before speaking. "Come on. Get in the car and let's go."

Hannah crossed her arms in front of her. "I'm not going anywhere until you answer my question." She raised her eyebrows expectantly while he took a few deep breaths.

"Hannah."

"Yes," she answered serenely, linking her hands together in front of her.

He sighed. "Get in the car because everyone from that stupid office is not-so-subtly staring at us through the window, and my foot feels like it needs to be amputated. So either plant a massive kiss on my lips right now or get in the car, okay?"

Hannah debated the kiss for a half a second. "Fine, let's go to your car," she said haughtily.

"I thought you'd see it my way," he said, grabbing her hand again and starting for his car. "Well, I didn't really have a choice, now did I?" Hannah huffed as they reached his Range Rover. Jackson braced his arm on the SUV, sheltering her from the view of the office. She could see from his eyes that he was still irate. He stood close enough that the wind was laced with his cologne, and she felt the heat of his breath on her as he spoke. She ignored the twinge of excitement that teased her at his nearness. Her body was a traitor to her mind.

"Oh, I gave you a choice, but you took the chicken's way out," Jackson whispered.

Hannah was about to open her mouth to make a smart reply when Santa jingled his way over to them. Santa, Hannah noticed with a frown, had a slight limp, a very disheveled appearance, and a tummy that looked like it had one too many beers in it. Jackson shoved a twenty-dollar bill at the man without taking his eyes off her. Santa rewarded him by jingling the bell in his ear. Hannah burst out laughing. Jackson cursed under his breath and opened the door for her. He grumbled something about small towns as he closed her door.

Five minutes later they were pulling up outside her home. It was the only place they could have complete privacy, but it was also a little unsettling to know that Jackson was now entering her territory. Her house was her own private sanctuary, the only home that had ever truly been hers.

Neither of them said anything on the way. Hannah knew that if she spoke she was only going to end up yelling at him, and considering that his hands were white as he gripped the steering wheel she figured he'd had about all he could handle at the moment. Which was fine, because now she was out of a job and she had Jean launching an all-out war against her and the adoption. She truly hoped Jackson was still as confident as he said he was about adopting Emily.

• • •

"This is your house?" Jackson asked, shutting the ignition and leaning forward to get a better look.

"This is it," she said, her voice still standoffish.

It had taken them only minutes to cross the little village of Hope's Crossing. From what he saw of the town, through his haze of red, was that it was that Norman Rockwell, picture perfect type of place. Cutesy, put-it-in-a-snow globe type of village. But he wasn't really interested in the town. His mind worked overtime trying to process everything. He felt like he was starring in some bizarre movie of himself. When had his life become so unpredictable?

He stared through the window at the red brick Victorian

before him and his throat constricted involuntarily. It was so damn idyllic. It was small, ornate. There was cedar roping with dark red ribbons that framed the heavy molding on the windows and the pristine white porch. Urns were overflowing with cedar and other greenery. The white plump snowflakes that floated down from the sky only made it more magical.

He actually found himself unable to speak for a moment because never in his life had something ever evoked in him such a need to have a home. A real home. A house. With a wife. With kids. Hell, maybe even a white picket fence. But Jackson Pierce was not your white picket-fence kind of man. No, he was the guy who lived in a penthouse surrounded by skylines and anonymity. Steel and glass. Money and ambition. Shallowness and greed. Loneliness.

"It may not be a mansion, Jackson, but it's perfect for me." He heard her unlatch her seatbelt and he knew she was seconds from jumping out of the SUV.

"It's you. Totally you." *It's beautiful, sentimental, nostalgic, pure Hannah.* Her cheeks bloomed with that gorgeous blush he found himself utterly hooked on and those lips that made him curse the fact that they'd never slept together that night.

"Oh," Hannah said, furrowing her brow and looking out the windshield.

"What, no smart-ass retort?" he teased, feeling better for a moment. Then he pictured some jerk's hands on Hannah and he felt the need to bash his fist through the windshield. So he frowned. And then she frowned back at him.

"Let's go inside and see how we can straighten out this mess you got us into." She didn't give him a chance to argue as the door shut on his reply. Funny how she was the one giving him the cold shoulder.

He followed her up to the covered porch. They had a lot of straightening out to do, all right. He braced himself for a hell of a battle. She was so damn secretive about her life he wondered how he could feel such an intense connection with someone he knew so little about. But he'd found out way more than he'd bargained for thanks to that Jean woman.

He waited while Hannah fumbled with the old lock. Moments later he stood in her entranceway while she walked around turning on lights. He was struck by the hominess. Feminine and cheerful, with pale yellow walls, deep trim and molding, and wide-plank pine floors scattered with brightly colored rugs. He followed her into the kitchen, where she had already started brewing a fresh pot of coffee. She took out cups and was banging things around a little too loudly.

"Hannah." His voice came out harsher than he intended, but he needed answers. He didn't want a cup of coffee and he didn't want to beat around the bush. "Care to tell me what that battle-axe was talking about back there?"

"What do you mean?" she asked stiffly, her shoulders squared, her back ramrod straight. A part of him wanted to cross the distance between them and knead the tension out of her slender shoulders, to whisper and coax whatever she hid out of her. But he knew she wouldn't respond to that. He knew that she would see it as being weak.

"Don't play games with me, Hannah."

"I don't play games," she said, whipping around to face him.

He nodded, softening his features, his tone, hating that he had to ask something that was already killing him to think about let alone speak about. "Hannah, she said you were beaten and almost raped." He watched as every single speck of color drained from her face. "What happened?" He caught a faint quiver in her chin when he spoke.

"That's what this is about…what you're angry about?" she asked, her voice shaky, her eyes wide and so heartbreakingly vulnerable that he just wanted to walk over and hold her. Hannah never let her vulnerability show, which meant...he clenched his stomach, not able to breathe at the thought... it confirmed what he already suspected...her reaction to things...the night he'd touched her arm...her withdrawal from him sexually.

"Jackson?"

He focused in on her pale face and nodded. "What did you think?"

"About your sister." She took a deep breath, her eyes filled with pain. "It's my fault that she killed herself. I missed the signs—"

"God, you can't blame yourself. Of course I don't blame you for that. How could anyone?" He walked across the room, unable to stop himself from offering her comfort. "Hannah," he said roughly, gathering her against him. "I could never blame you." His arms tightened around her. He felt all the tension leave her body, and she wrapped her arms around him. He wanted to reassure her, comfort her. How could she blame herself for Louise's death? How could she hold more guilt than he? He had failed his sister. Not Hannah. He kissed the top of her head, the soft hair at her temples, his hands moving to stroke that tender spot on her neck. He wanted to shut out the rest of the world and stay in this Victorian cottage.

"If anyone is to blame it's me. I'm the one who turned my back on her." He had never admitted that out loud. He had spent most of his adult life feeling angry at Louise, but deep down he knew he'd given up on her. He could have tried one more time. He felt Hannah take a steadying breath against him and slowly step out of his arms. Just like that, like a flurry of clouds suddenly taking away the sun, Hannah put distance between them.

She looked up at him and he wanted to know what she saw, uncomfortably aware that he hadn't given a damn in a long time what someone thought of him. Once he'd become wealthy and successful he'd thought that was all he needed. He had made it and nothing could touch him. But now, standing here in this tiny kitchen, with her beautiful face and glorious eyes staring up at him, he questioned all of it. Everything he had achieved, he wondered if it was enough.

"We all do what we have to do to survive. You gave her so much. No one can blame you for finally taking care of yourself." How did she do it? How could she see through him like that?

She turned to get the coffee.

"Hannah?"

"Mm-hmm," she murmured, stepping around him to pull out a carton of milk from the fridge, as though nothing had happened, as though they were merely casual acquaintances about to share a cup of coffee.

"You never answered my question." He caught the tremor in her hand as she poured the coffee. She was a master at avoidance.

"Are you hungry?" she asked, peering into her fridge.

He shut the fridge and she frowned up at him.

"You're not going to let this go are you?"

He shook his head.

"It's really not as dramatic as she made it sound," Hannah said, and he knew she was trying to act casual as she walked passed him to sit at the round table. He followed her, picking up his mug of coffee, sitting across from her at the table.

"So then it shouldn't be too difficult for you to talk about it," Jackson said, watching her eyes flash with annoyance. He took a sip of his coffee, his fingers gripping the handle tightly, waiting for her to speak. He was half expecting her to tell him she wasn't going to talk about it.

She cleared her throat after taking a long drink. "It was one of my first cases I'd been assigned to. She was a teenager, living with an abusive, alcoholic father. Long story short, when she didn't return my calls I found out she had gotten approval to get out of our system." She traced the rim of the smooth cup and he could tell she was getting lost in the memory. He felt his muscles tense in anticipation of where this story was going.

"I had a gut feeling that things didn't magically get better at home. So one night, I stopped by their place. I was a total rookie," she said with a small laugh that didn't hold an ounce of amusement. "I heard yelling. Men's voices. Then I heard Jen's voice, but it was more of a scream."

Jackson held his breath and waited for her to continue.

"At that point I should have called in for help, but I was young, and stupid, and I ran in there and, God, did I learn a lesson that night," Hannah said with laugh that was so self-critical, so deprecating that Jackson felt his throat tighten. She looked up at the ceiling, blinking back tears that she couldn't hide from him. "Her dad was gone and two of his friends had her pinned down on the sofa, half naked. And uh…I was no match for them," she said, turning her eyes to him. And at that moment he hated more than he ever thought he could hate someone. Hannah's eyes didn't leave his when she continued.

"They pushed me down before I could run, before I could think of how to defend myself. They laughed, they slapped me around, ripped my clothes. The harder I fought, the harder they laughed. They touched me and when I thought…when I thought that was it, Jen came up from behind and whacked the guy that was on top of me with a frying pan. We managed to knock the other one unconscious too. We ran out to my car and drove to the police station." Jackson was torn between wanting to hold her and wanting to smash something. He knew, based on her stiff posture, the tilt of her chin and her cool tone that she didn't want him to touch her. And he knew it was because she would lose it if he did. That stranglehold she had on her emotions would come undone.

But he couldn't sit still anymore. He couldn't get the image of Hannah being thrown on the ground and touched by those animals out of his mind. Jackson had lived through his own hell. He wasn't a naive man. But hearing this, hearing someone try and hurt someone so good, someone he cared for, made him want to go out and inflict some serious bodily harm.

"They didn't—uh—" How the hell could he finish that sentence? He gripped the side of the thick pine table as Hannah shook her head.

"No. And I have no regrets for going in there that night. If I hadn't gone in, they would have raped her, Jackson," she said, emotion returning to her eyes, softening her voice...and ultimately melting his heart. "I only regret not having a plan, walking in there by myself. The next morning I registered for self defense classes." He knew they were both thinking about that night in his bed, when she'd told him she could have knocked him to the ground. He almost wanted to smile with pride for her, for her strength and determination, and that unwavering courage. Then he thought of the last night when she was in his arms and had stopped him from making love to her. She was still afraid.

"What happened to them?"

Hannah shrugged. "Serving a ten year sentence."

"You know that wouldn't have happened if it weren't for you."

• • •

Hannah nodded absently. She felt warmed by the way he was looking at her, the admiration she heard in his voice. Hannah couldn't believe she had revealed so much. She hadn't spoken about that night in years. But somehow it felt right to tell him, to share that part of her. She had been acutely aware of his tension, had seen his knuckles turn white as she spoke. And try as she might to deny it, it felt so wonderful to have someone care for her. It was just like when he found her in the snow, when he spoke up to Jean for her.

"Hannah, about Emily."

Hannah felt her stomach flip flop. "You can raise her, Jackson, I know you can do it."

"But it would be better if I were married. I want every chance to win this. To get Emily forever."

Of course a married couple would be better but that didn't mean *her*. "While that is true, your case is solid—"

"Do you remember what you said to me this morning?"

Hannah shook her head slowly, even though what she had said was dawning on her.

He leaned forward so that there was barely any distance between them at the table. "You said you would do anything to help me."

Hannah's heart beat ferociously. "I think marrying you is a little beyond help."

"Look at it like a business arrangement."

He was nuts. He actually thought they should get married. He had gotten it into his undeniably handsome head that he was going to rescue his niece. Now he needed to figure out the logistics and she was the easiest solution.

"Business arrangement?"

"You and I get married. You move into my place, help me raise her. I'll pay you for your help."

"I can't let you pay me." Hannah crossing her arms across

her chest.

"Why not? You're providing me with a service."

"So am I the nanny slash housekeeper?"

"No, I want you to help me care for her. I have a housekeeper and cook already. I need you to guide me, and take care of the day to day stuff that a baby would need."

"How long is this arrangement for? Am I going to drop my life, sell my house, and move in indefinitely?"

"That's the gist of it. And you'll have enough time to continue school. I'll pay your tuition. I don't want you to give that up."

This was ridiculous. Hannah felt a nervous shiver creep up her spine as he stared determinedly at her. It was easy for him to say drop everything and leave. Her house, her home was everything to her. It was the first place that no one could take away from her and now…

"Hannah, I need you, Emily needs you." He needed her? It was wonderful to think that he meant her, but she knew of course he meant that he needed her for Emily. And Emily, how could she let go of the little baby that she already desperately loved?

"I couldn't possibly live with you though, you, you're… you're…"

"Handsome, rich, and irresistible?"

"Obstinate, arrogant, and domineering."

"Ah, but that's all a front."

"There's really a guy with a heart of gold under there?"

"Exactly."

"So, if I agree to this…"

"We go to city hall the day after tomorrow. I'll have my lawyers take over the adoption process. I'm not going to lose Emily. *We're* not going to lose her." Hannah believed him, but marriage? Living together? She had to think of it as a business arrangement. Emily would have a great home with her uncle. Hannah would be able to sleep at night knowing she'd fulfilled Louise's last wish, and she would get to be in Emily's life. What more could she want?

"In the meantime, if you want to get your things from your house, we'll lock it up, and get you settled into my place in the city," Jackson said, as casually as if he'd mentioned grabbing a sandwich for lunch.

Hannah stared blankly at him. "Now?"

He nodded. "I thought we had gone over this?"

"Settling into your place, like right away?"

"We're obviously going to have to live together in order to be the family we say we are to adopt Emily. This is your area of expertise, Hannah. I shouldn't be the one telling you how this works. We can come back here on the weekends or something."

Hannah felt her heart beat painfully. "Jackson. This is a *pretend* marriage. Once you get Emily, I'm out of the picture." She didn't realize those words would or could actually cause her pain. For a second she could see herself with Jackson and Emily, as a real family. But she'd never be the right woman for Jackson. What if one day, when his attraction to her wore off, he'd decide he didn't need her around? She couldn't let herself get attached to him, or the idea of being a real family.

"Hannah, what are you worrying about now?"

"In the span of two hours I lost my job, am getting married, adopting a baby, moving out of my house to God knows where—"

"My penthouse," he said with a laugh, "is not God-knows where. It's like an hour from here."

"Fine, so I'm leaving my little town for some playboy penthouse." She drummed her fingers against the table while he laughed.

"You really have got me all wrong don't you," he said, smiling.

"You did have that basket of female toiletries at the cabin."

His loud laugh interrupted her again. She glared at him.

"So you assumed that I bring hoards of women up to my cabin, seduce them, and then give them gift baskets?" His grin was starting to bother her, and so were his logical explanations. "You're the only woman who's been up to my cabin, Hannah," he said, his voice low and throaty. "That basket was left by the designer."

Her hands settled around her mug of cold coffee. "This is not easy. I haven't had time to process anything."

"Hey, who found who, remember?" he said gently. She stopped for a moment and took a deep breath. She had found him, and he was doing exactly what she'd wanted. Could she fault him for trying to make this all work? So what was the big deal to marry Jackson temporarily? Her stomach flopped over. Marry him. Sham or not, it was a huge deal.

"Why don't we take this one day at a time. Get your stuff, settle into my place, we get married. Help me set up for Emily's arrival, and then we'll see what happens."

"You know, I remembered that I really need to, um, do something. I'll be right back," Hannah said and bolted out of the room. She ran into her bedroom, feeling like a complete moron. She didn't hear him walk in and jumped at the sound of his voice. Jackson filled up her tiny bedroom like a lion in a dollhouse.

"Why are you running away from me?"

Her eyes went to the pile of Christmas presents she'd purchased for Emily. Perfect. She could get them ready. But when she started to turn, Jackson gently reached out to grab her wrist. She didn't try to pull away. His touch felt decadent, impossible to refuse.

"Why did you end things the other night?"

She felt her face ignite at the memory. Her eyes darted to her antique bed and she couldn't stop the image of the two of them sprawled across it. What was he doing to her? She finally looked up at him, and realized he stood way too close. And they were both standing way too close to her bed. Years of self-control and self-preservation could be easily tossed out the window when she stood this close to this man. And why did he have to look so good without a shave? It was that darn firm jaw, the eyes that were so…

"Why aren't you answering my question?"

Hannah looked up at him guiltily. "What was the question again?"

Then he smiled, that arrogant, mischievous smile that somehow didn't seem to bother her anymore. "The other night, when we were about to make love." His voice turned throaty and his fingers began circling her wrist.

"We weren't about to make love," she said shaking her head, lying through her teeth.

"Really?" he said, lowering his face to hers, probably to make sure she could see that he wasn't buying her innocent act for one second.

She shook her head. "Nope. It was just—"

"You can't claim it was the alcohol because you were within your own prescribed limit of intoxication."

She frowned. Damn him and his smug reminder.

She crossed her arms. "You're very amusing, Jackson." She had to pause since there was no use trying to speak over his laughter.

"One minute you're telling me deeply personal information and the next you're lying."

"I don't lie."

"So you don't think we were on our way to bed together that night?"

She forced herself to look up at him. "It was a momentary lack of judgment. You rescued me from a blizzard, so naturally—"

"You're a virgin, aren't you?"

Jackson Pierce had no discretion whatsoever. Hannah wished her ancient floor would give in and swallow her whole.

"What on earth makes you think that?"

"I'm starting to piece two and two together."

"Two and two makes four."

He took a step closer to her. Her body temperature rose by at least ten degrees. They needed to get off this topic and out of her bedroom.

"You know, your avoidance is only proving my theory," he said, again taking a step toward her. She refused to back up in case she looked cowardly, but his proximity made it even harder to ignore her attraction to him. "You're not usually a liar, but you are a master at avoidance."

Hannah sighed theatrically.

"So, I'll ask you again, Hannah. Are you a virgin?"

"Stop saying that stupid word," she said finally, emphasizing stupid with a poke into his rib cage.

He chuckled. Low and deep. She glared at him until he stopped.

"What word? Virgin?"

She sighed and nodded stiffly.

"Stop laughing at me."

"You think I'm making fun of you?"

She nodded.

He moved slowly and her breath caught in her throat as she watched his eyes take on that warmth that had the ability to turn her knees into jelly. He softly touched her face, his thumb grazing her lower lip. She felt a heat spread through her and was unable to stop herself from turning her face into the palm of his hand. And then, shocking both of them, she kissed his skin. She heard a low sound from Jackson's throat and then she was in his arms, feeling the solid heat of his body against hers. She felt her heart beating as rapidly as his. All she did was feel. He trailed kisses down her face until he reached her lips. Hannah wanted nothing more than to kiss him.

"You are the last person I would ever make fun of. Ever," he said in a low voice.

She felt her body melding into his as her arms wrapped around him.

"I've never had so much respect for another human being." It was sweet, sweet torture, hearing him say this to her and touch her. "God, you make me want things, Hannah." He groaned, shattering all her defenses. She returned his kiss with the same desire, the same understanding. She couldn't walk away from him, from this glimpse of heaven he offered. He offered himself, his niece—a family.

Jackson slowly pulled back, his eyes still dark with desire. Hannah felt her body tremble, felt the loss of not having his lips on hers.

"Marry me," he said gruffly, gently brushing her hair off her face.

Hannah felt her heart swell and she knew she couldn't say no anymore. She nodded, knowing that nothing would ever be the same.

Chapter Eleven

"Good morning, Mr. Pierce."

Jackson's pace slowed for a second, and he was vaguely aware that everyone in the office was trying their best not to stare at him. The offices of Pierce & Dane Software were situated on the top floor of one of the tallest buildings in downtown Toronto. Jackson and Ethan knew they'd made it the day they were able to purchase, staff, and run this office ten years ago.

"Morning, Ann," Jackson said with a nod, and resumed his fast pace towards Ethan's office. He gave a knock and walked in without waiting for a response. His friend looked up from his computer monitor, his mouth dropping open.

"What the hell are you doing here?"

"Nice to see you too." Ethan's office was next to his and nearly identical. A massive, modern mix of glass and steel with floor-to-ceiling windows framing the city's skyline.

Jackson sat down across from Ethan's desk with a thud, tossing his briefcase on the leather chair beside him. His friend continued to stare at him as though he'd grown a second head. Much like everyone had outside.

"It's December. You're never here," Ethan said, frowning.

"Oh, that," he said flatly. "I'm back because I'm getting married tomorrow."

Ethan shook his head and gave him a nervous laugh. "Sorry, I could have sworn you just told me you're getting married."

Jackson sighed and stretched out his legs on Ethan's desk, crossing them at the ankles. This was going to be fun. "You heard right. Tomorrow. Getting married."

Ethan leaned forward. "*You* are getting married?"

"Yup," Jackson said, noticing the interesting way the snow was falling in the windows behind Ethan. Funny, he'd never really noticed that. Had snow always looked that good from this high up?

"To *who?*"

"Someone I met."

"Did something happen to you? You are Jackson Pierce, right? Cold, self-centered, egotistical?"

"Hey, hey," he said holding up his hands. "Take it easy there. I'm not cold."

"Is it too early to drink?" Ethan mumbled walking toward the bar. Jackson wasn't sure if he should laugh, be insulted, or join him.

He waited for Ethan to sit back down. "Call Ann in here, would you?"

"Why?" Ethan said, looking even more worried than before. He noticed Ethan had opted for coffee instead of alcohol.

"I need her help with the wedding details," Jackson said, glancing down at his phone. He kept expecting Hannah to phone him saying she'd changed her mind.

Ethan swore loudly. "Wedding planning?"

Jackson scowled at his tone. "Yes. Either you get Ann in

here or I will."

Ethan rested his elbows on the desk. "First, you tell me what woman on earth agreed to marry you."

"You'll meet her tomorrow."

"Why am I meeting her tomorrow?" Ethan groaned, massaging his temples.

"Because that's the wedding," Jackson said with a rough sigh. Ethan gave him a look he'd never seen before and then marched back to the bar, this time reaching for the scotch instead of the coffee.

"Listen, buddy, you've been gone for a little over a week into your yearly three week pity-party—"

Jackson held up a hand. "It's not a pity-party. It's a man-cation."

Ethan gave him a long look. "Whatever makes you feel better. So, now you're back early, and you're telling me that you, the man that doesn't date the same woman more than three times, is getting married. *Tomorrow.* And this woman entrusted you to the wedding planning."

So maybe it sounded a little out of character for him. Jackson shrugged. "Change of plans."

"At least tell me how you met."

"She showed up at my door."

He ignored Ethan's loud curse. "And so you decided to marry the first woman that knocked on the door of that godforsaken cabin in the middle of nowhere? Did it ever occur to you that she's after your money? I hope you've had the common sense to have a pre-nup drawn. What kind of woman goes knocking on a stranger's door?"

Jackson leaned forward. "A very good woman, that's who. She's a social worker."

Ethan let out a huge sigh. "*Oh,* so she was there to council you."

"Not funny. Look. Long story short. My sister had—" Jackson cleared his throat past the odd lump that formed in his throat whenever he thought of Louise and Emily. "My sister had a baby before she died. And this woman—Hannah—was Louise's social worker. The most sure way for me to gain custody of the baby is by getting married." Ethan knew all about his screwed up family, including his relationship with Louise. Jackson shifted uncomfortably in his seat. Any sympathy from Ethan would be revolting and awkward.

Ethan looked up from his empty glass, and whispered hoarsely, "You're going to be a father, too?"

Jackson swore under his breath and leaned forward, pressing the button on Ethan's phone to connect him with Ann. This conversation had gone on long enough.

Ann marched brusquely into the room. "Mr. Pierce, how nice to see you this time of year," she said, sitting opposite him, notepad on her lap.

Jackson noted how formal and stiff her posture was. Did he make her nervous? Come to think of it, everyone around here was that way with him. When had that happened? Sure, Ethan had always been the easier going of the two of them, but when had people actually become intimidated by him?

"Thanks, Ann. Nice to see you as well. I have an odd project I need your help with," he said, trying to sound relaxed and pleasant as she set her pen to ready position, her head tilted in his direction.

"I'm getting married tomorrow." Jackson paused as Ann's wrist jerked to the side and drew a jagged line across the blank page. She quickly blushed and looked up, turning the page. Jackson ignored Ethan's not-so-subtle laugh and continued. "I need some help with the details."

Ann nodded, looking panicked.

"This is the address," he said, handing her a slip of paper.

"I need lots and lots of white and red roses. And green Christmas bushy type things."

Ann looked up at him in terror. Jackson tried to smile. "I trust you, Ann. Something nice."

She nodded slowly, her eyes darting toward Ethan. Ethan held up his hands and leaned back in his chair.

"Oh, and what are those branch things, with red berries on them?"

"Um, I think you mean hollies, Mr. Pierce."

Jackson snapped his fingers. "Yes, perfect. Some of those too. And candles," Jackson said, again ignoring the loud noises coming from Ethan's direction.

"Does Ann need to get the wedding dress too?" Ethan drawled.

Jackson scowled at him. "No, I'm getting that myself."

"Oh my God," Ethan said, shaking his head.

"Lastly, I need you to track down this couple near my cabin. Last name Sampson. Make sure they are at the wedding. Get a car for them or something. I don't think they can get there on a sleigh."

"What the hell went on at that cabin?" Ethan roared.

Ann looked nervously back and forth between them. Jackson ignored him.

"The wedding is at five o'clock. Okay? Got everything you need?"

Ann nodded slowly, and Jackson could tell she was trying her best not to ask any questions.

"Oh, Ann, one more thing. Did you give a woman my address to my cabin?"

Ann's white face went bright red, and her chin wavered. "I, uh, I'm so sorry, Mr. Pierce. She was so persuasive and she said that it was a matter of life or death."

Jackson swallowed his laugh. "Yes, I'm familiar with that

line. It's all right. Thanks for your help, Ann," he said, rising and walking across the room. He had a ton of stuff to get done today, he thought, mentally checking the *tell Ethan* item off his list. He stopped at the door and looked back at his friend and Ann.

"Ann, give everyone the day off tomorrow."

Ann looked from him to Ethan, her mouth hanging open. Ethan just shrugged.

"Ethan, make sure you're at that address by four o'clock tomorrow. You're my best man." With that he walked out of his office.

• • •

"I can't believe you're getting married," Allison said as Hannah slipped on her ivory heels in front of the full-length mirror at the entrance of her home.

Hannah shook her head. "Neither can I." She hadn't been able to sleep at all last night. All she could think about was her sham of a marriage that was about to happen. Of course, she understood they really had no choice if they wanted to adopt Emily. Did the thought of being Jackson Pierce's wife send a tingle up her spine? Well, yeah, fine. But that still didn't mean they were destined for a life-long marriage. She glanced over at Emily, who stared at her, sucking her pink pacifier. She smiled at the baby, laughing as Emily smiled back and the pacifier popped out. Looking at the adorable baby she had no doubts—she was about to secure Emily a real home. She was about to do what no one had ever been willing to do for her, and nothing, *nothing* mattered more than that.

"I didn't know Emily was coming with us," Allison said, crouching down to tickle Emily's toes.

"Neither did I. Mrs. Ford called this morning, saying that

Jackson had asked her if Emily could come to the wedding."

"Wow, she agreed on such short notice?" Allison asked, rising.

"He can be very persuasive," Hannah said, smoothing her hand over her simple winter-white suit. She bit on her lower lip as she stared at her reflection in the mirror. She looked like a woman about to attend a business meeting. Sure, her hair looked okay, she left it loose and allowed it to tumble naturally around her shoulders. That had nothing to do with the fact that she couldn't stop thinking about Jackson running his fingers through her hair. And the extra dab of lip gloss? Merely for the moisture protection against the harsh winter wind.

"And extremely hot," Allison said with a smirk.

Hannah refused to take the bait. She was already feeling torn—if Allison detected a glitch in her armor she was done for. "Who, Jackson? I guess if you're into that sort of look."

"Uh, if you're a living, breathing woman you'd be into that look. Don't even try to deny you're attracted to him, Hannah. You never did tell me what went on at that cabin."

Hannah frowned. "I spent all my time trying to convince him to adopt Emily. I told you, we are only doing this for Emily. That's it."

"Mm-hmm," Allison said, her sly smile turning into a wide, I-don't-believe-one-word-of-this grin.

"I barely even know the man," Hannah said, grabbing her purse and avoiding eye contact.

"Really? It certainly looked like you two knew each other, I mean the way he gallantly rescued you."

"He rescued his *niece*. That's it."

"I know you, Hannah. There's way more going on here," Allison said, the teasing in her voice gone.

Hannah tucked her hair behind her ear. "I don't know

what to tell you. He's different from anyone I've ever met. And he's got major issues. But there's something," she said, trying to put into words something she really didn't understand herself. "He makes me feel safe and scared at the same time. That sounds crazy, doesn't it?"

"No, that kind of sounds like love," Allison whispered.

Hannah brushed off the notion. She couldn't love anyone like that and she was wise enough to know that no one would love her like that. Her dreams of happily-ever-after, they were only that—dreams.

Gravel crinkling under the weight of an approaching car allowed Hannah to escape any more questions. Allison's eyes locked on hers like a deadbolt before running over to the window, pushing aside the curtain. "Well, well, a black Audi stretch limo."

Hannah swallowed nervously and felt her face getting warm. Had Jackson done that? He hadn't told her he'd be sending a limo.

"Now I wonder who could have done that? The tall, dark, handsome man who's about to be your husband?" Allison asked, tapping her manicured finger on her chin, not even trying to contain her grin. "And here comes the driver." Allison whipped open the front door before the man could ring the bell.

"Ms. Woods?" the straight-faced man asked to neither lady in particular.

"She's right over there," Allison said, holding the door open even wider.

"Yes," Hannah said with a glare at Allison.

"I'm here to take you to the chapel," he said graciously, extending his arm in the direction of the waiting limo.

Hannah's eyes darted from the shiny black limo to the man. "Chapel?" They were supposed to meet at City Hall. As if sensing Hannah's confusion the driver slipped an envelope out of the interior pocket of his pristine black coat.

"Ms. Woods, this is from Mr. Pierce," he said with a smile, handing her the white envelope. Hannah gave her friend a shake of the head and turned around for privacy. Thick, black bold script stood out on the pristine white card.

Hannah, change of plans. Meet me at the chapel instead. Jackson.

And then, as if he anticipated her reaction, he had scribbled *"Please"* underneath. Hannah felt her heartbeat begin to race. Marrying at a chapel instead of City Hall was starting to sound much more like a real wedding than merely a formality. Why would he do this? Why wasn't he keeping this a simple business arrangement like they'd planned? She clutched the note until the corners began to curl. Fear held her prisoner, shackled her feet to the floor, burying her in quicksand filled with dire warnings.

"So, let's go get this sham of a marriage done, huh, Hannah," Allie said with a laugh, jolting Hannah back to the moment. She blinked, forcing herself to move. Allison grabbed Emily inside the car seat and dragged Hannah onto the front porch.

"Not funny, Allie." She silently cursed Jackson as they followed the driver to the waiting limo. Maybe she could try texting him on the way to the chapel, demanding some sort of explanation. And then she realized she didn't even have his number. Who gets married to someone when you don't even have their cell phone number?

"Stop panicking and get in the limo," her friend said laughing, while Hannah stood beside the car. Hannah nodded. She was setting herself up for heartbreak, she realized as she sank into the plush leather seats of the limo.

• • •

A little over an hour and what felt like five hundred questions later, the limousine purred to a stop outside a white, clapboard chapel. It was nestled in the countryside, surrounded by snowy hills and towering trees, whose branches were heavy with mounds of snow. Even though they were only half an hour north of the city, it felt as though they were miles away. The area wasn't familiar at all, Hannah thought, looking through the windows. There were three vehicles in the parking lot. The only one she could identify was Jackson's Range Rover.

"How pretty. This is right out of a Trisha Romance painting," Allison whispered, her face practically pressed against the window.

They stepped out onto the freshly shoveled and salted pathway that led up to the chapel. Hannah grew more and more apprehensive with every step they took. The driver held open the door of the chapel and Hannah's breath caught in her throat and she had to set the car seat down. She really didn't know Jackson Pierce at all.

White and red roses and sprigs of holly and cedar in elegant silver buckets lined the aisle and adorned the altar. Candelabras and votives with ivory candles cast a warm, romantic glow. The tiny church was at least a hundred years old, simple but nostalgic and charming, and utterly breathtaking.

"This way, ladies," a woman called out to them, and Hannah tore her eyes from the empty altar in the direction of the voice. A woman she didn't recognize smiled at them as though they'd all been lifelong friends. Elderly and stately she waved them over to a room at the end of a corridor.

"Let's go," Allison said, grabbing her hand and the baby,

as though she knew Hannah was ready to bolt for the door. "We'd better hurry," Allison whispered, a smile in her voice. "The wedding that's purely a formality looks as though it's going to start soon."

Hannah felt a knot begin to form in her stomach. She couldn't do this. She couldn't go through with a pretend marriage that looked so…real. This wasn't City Hall; this was where two people who were in love got married.

They followed the silver-haired woman into a small room. The smell of roses made it feel as though they were in a garden on a warm July afternoon. There were dozens of them in silver bucket vases. Hannah's panic level got close to a breaking point. The woman stood in the center of the room and smiled at her.

"Hello, ladies, my name is Gwendolyn, and I'm Minister Holbrook's wife," she said. "He will be performing the ceremony today."

"Hello," Hannah and Allison said in unison. Hannah felt like they were two children as they both let the woman take charge.

"Oh my God," Allison gasped, clutching Hannah's arm and pointing toward something.

There was a dress, no a gown. There was an ivory beaded, full length gown hanging on a mahogany cheval mirror. Hannah's eyes lingered over the exquisite beading that twinkled under the lights, noting the graceful flow, the obvious hand-detailing. It was, simply put, the most exquisite thing she'd ever laid eyes on.

"Oh my God," Allison said again.

"What is this?" Hannah whispered, walking towards the gown, feeling something like a cross between Cinderella and Alice in Wonderland. Hannah reached out to feel the silk and beads crunch lightly between her fingertips. She quickly dropped her hand, feeling guilty, like a child caught stealing from the cookie jar. Perhaps it was that bit of little girl in her, the one who had never been given anything so special by anyone, or maybe it was the woman in her, the one who never thought she'd ever wear a dress like this. It felt too good for her.

. . .

"I can't wear this," Hannah said, shaking her head. She wasn't going to play whatever game Jackson had going on. She couldn't pretend to be a real bride.

"My dear, would you mind letting the groom know that you and Hannah have arrived?" the minister's wife said with a calm smile as she nudged Allison out of the room. Allison, for the first time since Hannah had met her, actually didn't have anything to say. Mrs. Holbrook shut the door and turned to look at Hannah.

Hannah shook her head when the woman approached her.

"I need to speak with Jackson, this wasn't what I agreed to—"

"I've known Jackson since he was a baby," Mrs. Holbrook said. She closed the distance between them, a serene smile in place, and began unbuttoning Hannah's coat. Hannah was too shocked by the woman's boldness to say anything. The woman had a very authoritative presence, but also calming, soothing.

"Every Sunday he would come to church with his mother and his sister," she said, draping Hannah's coat over an armchair. Hannah tried to picture Jackson as a child. "He always held his mother's hand and helped with his little sister. He was such a handsome little thing even then, big brown eyes and a mop of brown hair on his head. Sometimes his eyes twinkled with mischief, but when his mother got sick, they lost their spark." Hannah felt a lump start in her throat and didn't protest when the woman began taking off her suit jacket.

"His mother was a wonderful woman—strong and kind and loving. She loved her children with everything she had, right up until the end. And you know, Jackson," she whispered, and Hannah could have sworn she saw the woman blink back tears as she helped Hannah out of her clothes. Hannah held her breath, barely caring that she stood in the room in only her underclothes. Mrs. Holbrook took the gown off the hanger. "Jackson would walk his mother into church every Sunday. And when she was too sick to walk, he would wheel her in, holding his sister's hand at the same time." She slipped the gown over Hannah's head with a cool swoosh of silk, but Hannah barely noticed while she listened, trying to process this glimpse into Jackson's past. The woman zipped up the dress in a swift, gentle motion and Hannah felt it cling as though it had been custom made for her.

"The last time I saw Jackson was at his mother's funeral. Only ten years old, and I'll never forget his face that day. Buckets of tears poured from his eyes, but he didn't utter a sound, just held his sister. That was the last time I saw him, until the other night, when he knocked on my door, telling me about you, about Emily, about his sister."

The woman slowly turned Hannah around to face the full-length mirror. She held Hannah's gaze in the mirror, her eyes sincere. "He told me how brave you are, that you were very special," she whispered softly, smiling gently as Hannah's eyes filled with tears. Jackson had said that about her? She barely even recognized her reflection. Who was this woman with emotion glittering her eyes, making them sparkle and shine? And the dress... The straps sat on her bare shoulders and highlighted her creamy skin, the front of the gown dipped low, much lower than she would have dared, but she had to admit looked good as it clung to curves she normally kept hidden. It fit her waist like a glove and then slowly tapered out to a flowing A-line. Jackson had chosen this for her?

"You look wonderful, my dear." The woman beamed and Hannah truly felt like Cinderella at that moment. Would it be so bad to allow herself this fantasy? Would it be so horrible to enjoy this gorgeous gown? She thought of the night in her room, when he'd whispered to her, *I've never had so much respect for another human being…marry me tomorrow, Hannah.* She felt a delicious shiver tease her bare arms. She was fooling herself if she thought they were doing this purely for business.

"And this adorable little baby," she said kneeling down in front of Emily, "this must be Louise's little girl." The baby stared at her, wide-eyed, blue eyes fixed on the woman's smile. And when Hannah thought that Jackson couldn't do anything else to surprise her, Mrs. Holbrook opened the small closet behind Emily and took out an angelic ivory silk dress with tiny pink rosebuds around the waist.

"This is what Jackson picked out for this little dear," she said, holding the dress out to Hannah.

"Jackson picked this for her?"

Mrs. Holbrook nodded. "Yes, he picked them both out. He said when he saw your dress in the window of the custom shop he knew it was you. He was a little hesitant about Emily's dress, asking me if it was the right size." Mrs. Holbrook was already unclasping Emily's seatbelt in the car seat, as if she knew Hannah was incapable of moving.

"I don't know what he's doing," Hannah whispered, not really to anyone.

"Jackson knows exactly what he's doing, Hannah. You are

what he needs, my dear," the woman said with a reassuring smile, standing and holding Emily in her arms. "And soon you'll realize that Jackson is exactly what you need."

· · ·

Jackson felt nerves...no, *fear*, for the first time in a long, long time as he stood at the altar. Would Hannah tell him to go to hell? Did she walk out of here as soon as she realized he'd changed plans on her? Would she like the dress?

That day after he dropped Hannah off at home, as he drove back into the city, he couldn't shake the feeling that getting married at City Hall was wrong. For Hannah it was wrong. He wanted her to have everything, the best of everything. After what she'd told him at her house, about her past, he wanted her to feel special. He tried hard to tell himself that it was merely attraction to a beautiful woman, but he knew it was a lie. If that were true he wouldn't have contacted the Holbrooks. He wouldn't have bought the dress that he knew would fit Hannah like a glove, because he'd memorized every single inch, every luscious curve of her body. He wouldn't have picked the only chapel that held such significance to him. He never would have let her into this part of his past.

"Jackson, man, you look like you're about to hurl." Ethan laughed, slapping him on the back. Jackson bit back a curse as he glared at the man he considered his best friend. Ethan, it seemed, had gotten over his shock since yesterday. Today he was just overly irritating, asking him questions involving feelings. He wasn't about to enter into that discussion with a guy who had an even worse record with women than he did.

"I'm not going to hurl, you idiot," he said, straightening his tie, wondering if that was what the unsettled feeling in his stomach meant.

His friend rolled back and forth on his heels, way too happily. "Have you been drinking?"

Ethan scowled at him. "No. But who are those people that keep waving at you?" Ethan whispered under his breath.

Jackson forced a smile and waved at Mr. And Mrs. Sampson. "Friends of the bride."

"Who's that?" Ethan said as a pretty, slender brunette stood at the top of the aisle, then began walking toward them.

"Hannah's best friend, Allison. They work together. And hands off. She's not your type." Jackson said out of the corner of his mouth as Allison approached them.

"What's that supposed to mean?"

"She's nice," Jackson said in a low voice.

"Hannah will be out in a minute," Allison said with a big smile. Jackson tried not to let his relief show.

"Thanks," he said, his eyes shifting from hers to the back of the chapel. Allison gave him a small wink and then walked away.

Hannah was at the top of the aisle and was more beautiful than he imagined, a cross between an angel and a goddess. He couldn't read the expression in her eyes, but he bet she was torn between fury and confusion. His heart tightened as Allison and Emily made their way down the aisle. Little Emily evoked such an overwhelming feeling of love in him that he was taken aback.

Jackson heard the elderly minister of his youth shuffle across the altar to join him. He gave Jackson a reassuring nod, so similar to the one he gave when Jackson was a boy, coming to church with his mother and sister. He'd turned his back on his faith for so many years. But yesterday on that drive, after being with Hannah and his niece, he'd felt an inexplicable pull here, as though this place could bring him back to a time of peace and serenity. Everything around him faded as Hannah walked down the aisle, a simple bouquet of ivory roses in her hand.

. . .

Hannah was barely aware of anything other than Jackson. And boy, was the man a sight to behold. Tall and lean, wide shoulders and proud stance, he was a man who could stop traffic. He stood in a dark grey suit waiting for her, watching her with eyes that glittered with emotion. She saw a hint of that vulnerability as the corner of his mouth turned up. As soon as she stood beside him he took her hand in his.

"This isn't city hall, Jackson."

He chuckled softly, making her forget all the reasons this was insane. "City hall is too ordinary for you, Hannah," he whispered gruffly, giving her hand a squeeze. "You look beautiful."

"The Sampsons are here," she said, squeezing his hand.

The smile he gave her was one she wouldn't forget. "I know how fond you are of them. The only problem is that they think I'm deaf, so they've been yelling from the aisle." Hannah swallowed her nervous laugh and stared at him for a moment longer, not believing that this was the same man as a week ago.

This was a real wedding, she thought, as the minister began to speak. Words floated through the air, and Hannah heard herself make promises to a man whose gaze told her that he took this very seriously. When he spoke his vows, in that deep, self-assured voice, every ounce of insecurity dripped away. And when it was time to exchange rings, Jackson retrieved two rings out of his pocket before she even had a moment to panic. He had a slight smile as he smoothly slipped her ring on her finger. She looked down at the band, marveling at the beauty of the graceful filigree and shimmering diamonds. Then he handed her his wide, simple white gold band. Her hands trembled as she slid it onto his finger, their symbol of unity.

Finally, Jackson leaned down and gave her the sweetest, gentlest kiss that brought tears to her eyes and made her clutch his arms.

"Hello, Mrs. Pierce," Jackson whispered against her lips.

She squeezed his arms, feeling the dense muscles under her fingertips. "I never said I was changing my last name."

Jackson laughed and kissed her again.

The Sampsons, Ethan, and Allison were clapping. Hannah even thought she heard jingling bells. Emily picked that moment to thrill them with her own squeal of delight. This was the closest she had ever felt to having a family, Hannah thought, as the three of them stood together.

And if this were as close as she got, she'd die a happy woman.

Chapter Twelve

Jackson held the door for her with one hand, and carried her luggage with the other. Hannah gave him a small smile before walking by him and into his penthouse. He placed her bag on the ground and flicked on a table lamp in the foyer. Hannah ignored the jittery feeling in her stomach that had accompanied her from the church to the city. They had dropped Emily off at Mrs. Ford's house knowing that next week they'd be able to bring her home with them. The drive had been quiet, most of the joy of the wedding slowly replaced by nerves as the reality that she was about to move in with Jackson set in.

"Come on, I'll show you around," Jackson said, his deep voice sounding loud in the silent penthouse. He took her hand, leading her inside. She was curious to see his home, nervous to be here with him like this. The main lights were still off, the room illuminated by a breathtaking view of the Toronto skyline that twinkled through the gleaming ten foot windows. It was an impressive room, filled with leather, glass, and dark woods. Stunning, but impersonal, cold, and nothing like the man she was coming to know.

"What do you think?" He loosened his tie as he stood in the center of the room.

Hannah was having a hard time coming up with a smart answer, distracted by the way he looked. The image of his body intertwined with hers at the cabin gripped her. She remembered the exact shade of his skin, his masculine scent, each clearly defined muscle, and how glorious he'd felt against her naked body.

"Hannah?"

She attempted a casual smile and forced her eyes away from his before she turned red. "It's what I imagined it would be."

"Why doesn't that sound like a compliment?"

"It's, um…" She bit on her lip. "How do I put this? It's a very nice place for someone like you." *There.*

His smiled deepened and she resisted the urge to curl her toes. His smile should come with a warning attached. Allison's words about his looks popped into her mind and she quickly darted her eyes away from his. This evening was going to be more awkward than she'd originally thought, and they hadn't even had a tour of the bedrooms yet.

"Someone like me?"

"Well, no that's wrong, actually," she said, frowning as he removed his jacket. The long, lean lines of his body were perfectly outlined in the tailored suit. He was a beautiful man. She'd known that at the cabin. But seeing him dressed like this reminded her of the other side of him—the successful, powerful millionaire.

"You feeling okay?"

"Hmm?" She tore her eyes away and tried to remember what they were talking about. She took off her heels, absently touching the beading on the glorious dress he picked for her. He'd told Mrs. Holbrook she was special.

"I think you were getting ready to insult me," he said, walking over to a liquor cabinet. When he gave her that boyish grin again, the image of him as a child, helping his mother into church with Louise beside them, sprang into her mind. Hannah pictured him a few mornings ago, telling her he was going to adopt Emily. And then she thought of him today, in the chapel that he'd filled with flowers, looking more handsome than anyone she'd ever seen.

"Hannah?" He said again, his voice rough.

"I was trying to come up with something clever," she said, tears filling her eyes as worry furrowed his brow. She took a deep breath and spoke the most truth she'd ever spoken to anyone, throwing away her fear of rejection. "Thank you for today. Thank you for this dress," she said, trying not to be alarmed that his eyes glimmered with emotion she'd never seen before. *Do it, Hannah. Say it.*

"Thank you for making me feel special." She breathed in a huge gulp of air, trying not to cry. She wasn't going to hide from him, she thought, lifting her trembling chin. This one man had made her feel more important, and more cherished, than anyone she'd ever known.

•••

Jackson stopped breathing because suddenly there was no air in the room. All he needed to breathe was her. His chest throbbed with an unfamiliar, all consuming ache. Damn, she had the power to bring him to his knees. She took away all the blame he imposed on himself, and healed him. She saw something in him that made him feel good, and he thanked a God he hadn't spoken to in decades for her.

Jackson took her soft face in his hands, because he was incapable of not touching her. He refused to hide his feelings anymore, he needed her, and he was sure that in her own way she needed him. He had told himself that he wouldn't touch her tonight. He'd wait for her to come to him, but her words, her candor shook him to the core.

"Thank you." He paused, her eyes not leaving his, her body tense. "Thank you for banging down my door, for saving me and Emily." Her soft skin was cradled in his hands and he knew there would be no going back tonight. He read the desire on her face, in the rise and fall of her chest, and knew she wanted him as badly as he wanted her. "You make me want to believe, Hannah. In all of it." He took her mouth with his.

"I trust you, Jackson." Her words sent the blood pumping through his body even faster. She opened her mouth, her tongue greeting him instantly, and he groaned with her sweet surrender. She molded herself to him and it felt as though hers was the only body he'd ever known. He felt her hands at the nape of his neck, and then lower, touching his chest, his arms.

• • •

Hannah felt him suck in his breath as her hands skimmed over him, loving the feel of him, the ripple of muscle. He groaned deep in his throat and picked her up, her legs straddling him in a way that made her wonder how she was capable of doing this and not being afraid. But he made her forget all thought, all memories. He made her *feel*. As his lips worshipped her skin, her mouth, her lips, and as his strong hands worshipped her body, the only thoughts were of pure, sweet need. She needed Jackson, needed to be with him, to have him fill that void that had been missing her entire life.

"Jackson," she said. His hand cupped her breast. He didn't

answer, just made a throaty sound while his thumb grazed her nipple. And when she gasped against his mouth with pure delight, he cupped her bottom, lifted her higher against him, and dipped his head to make love to her nipple through the dress.

"Oh," she moaned out loud, not even realizing she spoke and clutched his shoulders. She heard him curse and the next thing she knew she was in his arms, his mouth still locked onto hers and he carried her into a large bedroom lit by the glow of the skyline. He placed her on the bed, and Hannah reached out to pull him down to her, unable to bear any distance between them. She'd spent her life not knowing of his existence and now the tiniest of seconds without him was torture.

He slid her dress off. She fumbled with the buttons on his shirt. He unhooked her ivory lace bra and lowered his body onto hers. Hannah thought she'd never felt anything so erotic as his powerful chest against hers, until he bent his head and captured her nipple in his mouth, licking and sucking until all she could do was whimper his name, arching her back off the bed, needing more.

"God, you are so beautiful, Hannah," he said, his lips trailing kisses and words of praise down her hot skin. She gasped. He kissed her at the top of her underpants, watching her. She nodded and he gave a low moan, wriggling out of her underwear, until she was completely naked before him. She didn't feel an ounce of fear. With him she was safe. His touch caressed her, telling her with his hands and with kisses how much he desired her, how much he cared for her, when he couldn't utter the words. And when she tugged at his pants and he was naked on top of her, all she could think of was him entering her, filling her with himself, healing her, loving her.

"In all my life, I've never seen or tasted anything as beautiful as you," he said in a low growl, licking and kissing his way down her body. All she could do was clasp his head to her and pray he never stopped. She didn't realize that she'd said that aloud until she heard his muffled laugh.

"Believe me, if I die, this is how I want to go." He touched her, tormented her inside with his fingers and for the first time she felt herself coming undone. He lay on top of her, his fingers increasing their erotic, insistent rhythm until she was arching against him. "Hannah," he whispered in a tortured breath, "reach for it, sweetheart. I've got you." And Hannah did, coming apart beneath him in wave after wave of sweet surrender. When she slowly began to resurface she reached for him, knowing that this wasn't enough, she wouldn't be complete without him.

"You're sure?"

She nodded, grasping his hips against hers. He entered her, slowly and gently, bracing himself on his forearms. Hannah knew it was killing him to be so controlled. She tucked her head into his shoulder, her hands slowly traveling the length of him until she cupped his firm buttocks. "Come inside, Jackson, please," she said, and finally he swiftly entered her fully. The pain was short, sweetness taking over until all Hannah could do was clutch him to her. His thrusts continued and continued. She cried out his name, digging her nails into his back, never imagining she could feel this way. Complete abandon, complete withdrawal from the person she thought she was to this…sweet heaven and both surrendered to their passion together.

• • •

Jackson stared down at the woman sleeping so peacefully in his arms and wondered how his life had seemed meaningful before her. He hadn't been living for anyone but himself, and now he was living for her and Emily. He bent to kiss the top of her head, the gesture coming so naturally to him when it never had before. He heard her soft sigh and a tiny smile appeared at one corner of her luscious mouth. She curled deeper into him and continued sleeping. He didn't think anything had ever felt so damn right as it did right now, with Hannah in his arms and Emily's adoption being processed. Nothing would ever come between them.

The vibration of his BlackBerry on the nightstand beside him sounded loud and harsh. He gently untangled himself from Hannah and reached for his phone. It was his lawyer, Nicholas Wright. He, Nick, and Ethan had all gone to college together and Nick was someone he considered to be a good friend as well as the best lawyer in town. Jackson stood, pulling the duvet over Hannah, and shrugging into his boxers. He left the room, answering the call as he shut the door.

"Jackson, I'm sorry to call you so late. I've been trying to reach you all day," Nicholas said, his voice sounding no more grim than usual.

"Yeah, I was busy getting married, remember?" Jackson said dryly, standing in front of the windows in the living room.

"Good, good. And that went well?"

Jackson chuckled. "Well, she didn't leave me at the altar, so I guess that's a good sign."

When he didn't hear his friend laugh on the other end, he knew it was serious.

"I don't know how to tell you this, but child services was contacted by a man claiming to be Emily's father."

Emily's father. Those words ricocheted through his body until he felt ill. "There is no father," he whispered raggedly, looking over his shoulder at the closed bedroom door.

"We don't know that it's her father for sure. We'll check this out, get the paternity tests done. There's no reason to panic."

"Who is he, Nick? If he was with my sister, he's an addict. He's probably after money. We can buy him off—"

"We have to do this by the book if we want to secure permanent custody. He's not in town. We'll know more when he gets here."

"My sister didn't know anyone that was decent enough to be able to raise a child. You have the note Louise left. It has my name on it. I'm that baby's family," he said, his hand tightening painfully around the phone.

"I know, I know. Like I said, don't panic yet. This could be nothing. I just wanted you to be aware of what was happening."

Jackson took a deep breath, thinking of the woman sleeping in his bed. She finally trusted him. He wasn't going to let her down. He wasn't going to let his niece down, or his sister. He'd been given a second chance and no one would get in the way of that.

"Keep me posted." He threw his phone onto the couch and ran his hands down his face with a sigh. What was he going to tell Hannah? He played out each scenario in his head and guilt ripped through him. But seeing Hannah's gorgeous face filled with pain over something that might not even be real made the decision easier for him. He wasn't going to tell her anything. It might just be a false alarm. Why should he get her worried for no reason?

He stared out the window and then at his reflection. His mother was dead. His father was dead. His sister was dead. It was just him and Emily. They were family and he could never let her go now. Feelings of protectiveness ignited a part of him he thought had been dead after Louise. No one was going to come in and threaten the life they were going to build.

Jackson paused at the doorway of the bedroom, watching Hannah sleep. Peaceful. Beautiful. He hated that he was going to lie, knowing it was the only way to keep her from pain. But the serenity on her face reinforced that he was making the right decision by not telling her. She deserved happiness.

She opened her eyes, and his gut clenched as she immediately looked over for him.

"Hi," he said walking into the room, pushing aside his guilt. He was doing this for her, that's all he had to remember.

"That was better than I ever thought possible," she whispered.

Jackson smiled, startled by her candor. He climbed into bed next to her, kissing her smooth shoulder. He felt goose bumps rise on her soft skin.

"Oh, I knew this was possible." He inhaled her fragrant skin, unable to keep his hands and mouth off her.

"Do you remember that day at the cabin when you found my stash of books?" she asked, completely taking him by surprise. He nodded.

"I started reading romance a long time ago." The corner of her mouth curled upward slightly, but somehow he knew it wasn't the smile of a person about to recount a happy tale of their youth. Maybe because he felt like he knew her so well already, or maybe it was because he understood that posture, that rueful smile, as one he'd practiced many times.

"I started out a lot like Emily," she said softly. "I was left in the cold, on a church doorstep, except there was no uncle, no long-lost relative, so I entered the foster care system."

Jackson couldn't breathe, couldn't think. He watched her blink rapidly, her eyes focused on the ceiling. It all clicked together so quickly, he wondered how he'd missed it.

"All I remember is never feeling loved. I didn't have much I could call my own. I didn't have a house, parents, anyone or anything..." Hannah paused for a moment and Jackson used every ounce of self-control to not say anything, to let her continue speaking. "Everything I had was in a suitcase, ready to be packed in case it was time for me to move to another home. I never had anything that was truly mine until I bought my house."

Jackson clenched his teeth, angry on her behalf, hurt for her.

"When I was old enough to realize that I could get out of the system as an adult, that's what I concentrated on. But there were times, depending on which foster home I was in, that getting out of the system seemed too far away. Some foster homes were better than others."

He heard the catch in her voice and caught the faint tremble in her chin, but she continued on, telling him things that he wished to God she'd never had to endure. "And then on my way home from school one day, I passed by the library and they were having a used book sale. I stopped at a pale purple book, and the title on the spine was *A Kingdom of Dreams*. And from the moment I opened that book until I shut it, I was a goner. It took me to a place where love conquered all, where men were honorable and—" She paused for a moment and he suspected when she cleared her throat it was to stop the tears. He waited for her to finish, feeling his own tension at her words, imagining her as this young teenager who learned to believe in happily-ever-after.

"The heroine actually got her kingdom in the end—her knight, his love." She touched his cheek, then pulled him down to her, and he kissed her, met and understood her need for him because it matched his own.

He pushed aside his guilt again—he was protecting her. He'd make everything right for her, for all of them. As their bodies melded, Jackson vowed that one day he'd give Hannah her kingdom.

Chapter Thirteen

"Would you like to help?"

He shook his head quickly to be safe. He had absolutely no idea what Hannah was up to. He'd gotten home from work, and instead of greeting Hannah at her usual post, amidst a stack of psychology books, she was in the kitchen. She looked sexy as hell in jeans and a snug-fitting sweater, her hair up in a ponytail and her cheeks rosy from…he had no idea what.

"I'd help you if I knew what you were doing," he said, planting a kiss on her soft lips.

"Excellent!" Hannah said, and thrust an apron in his direction. "I'm *baking*, Jackson. It's almost Christmas and we don't have any treats in this house," she said, sidestepping him to take out a tray of cookies from the oven.

"Is Emily sleeping?" His love for Emily had been the most unexpected realization. Not duty or obligation, but love. It had sort of snuck up on him when he was holding her or talking to her, and when Hannah had brought her to the office for a surprise visit, and Emily had spit up all over Ethan's desk because she'd been so excited to see Jackson.

Hannah nodded. "Yup, but she should be waking up

soon."

"Do babies eat cookies?"

"No, babies don't eat these." She frowned at him. "Have you heard anything from Nicholas?"

His heart slammed painfully. Jackson shook his head. "No, but everything should be finalized by the end of the week. You know all this, Hannah. I'm next of kin, we're married, and financially stable, and even our visit with the caseworker was perfect." So far, Emily's supposed father hadn't even shown up. Nicholas agreed it was probably some desperate attempt by a junkie to get some money.

She nodded, biting her lower lip. "I'll feel better once everything is signed and she's ours. It's always bothered me that Emily's father is MIA."

Jackson's mouth went dry. "We are her parents." In the last two weeks, living with Hannah and Emily had entrenched his determination to make legal what he knew in his heart to be true. There was no way in hell he'd allow someone to come in here and take away the family they were building together.

Hannah smiled at him. "You're right."

"Just hang tight."

His stomach growled loudly and he made a beeline for the tray filled with cookies. Hannah laughed and held up her hand, blocking him.

"No way. You have to help me. And besides, these haven't been decorated yet," she said, carefully placing each cookie, one by one, on a cooling rack.

"What about these?" He picked up a box filled with red sparkly cookies.

Hannah pried the box from his hands. "Those are for Ethan. Bring them into the office tomorrow," she said, placing the lid on the box.

"Why are you making Ethan cookies?"

Hannah sighed and adjusted her apron. He tried not to get distracted. He should just take that apron off.

"Because he called here a few minutes ago. I mentioned I was baking Christmas cookies and he asked if I could make some for him."

"Ethan? My business partner?" Jackson didn't think he'd ever seen Ethan eat a cookie.

She nodded, hands on her hips. "Apparently he likes red sprinkles."

"Red sprinkles?"

She nodded, this time a smile breaking. "Yes."

"He doesn't need cookies. Ethan grew up with a slew of nannies and housekeepers and cooks. I, on the other hand, was just a poor, neglected boy, so the cookies are mine," he said, laughing as Hannah shook her head. It was the first time he'd ever joked about his childhood.

"All right, Tiny Tim, roll up your sleeves and help me make these."

"I don't know anything about cookies, except eating them."

"You afraid?"

Her hands were in the bowl and the batter looked thick and doughy. He was not one to back down from a challenge. "You're the one who should be afraid," he said, smiling as she laughed. He took off his suit jacket and rolled up his sleeves. Evidently, he'd do anything for her.

"So what do I do?"

"We're going to roll this out and then make different Christmas shapes. Since you don't have any cookie cutters, we have to make them by hand."

He frowned. "Christmas shapes?"

He watched as she rolled the dough until it was thin and smooth. She let out an exasperated sigh. "Christmas trees, bells, angels, you know, anything *Christmas-y*."

"Right," he said with a decisive nod. He grabbed a piece of the dough and concentrated on making a tree, while the sound of Christmas songs floated into the kitchen. Before Hannah, not one Christmas carol had ever been heard in his penthouse.

"What *is* that! That looks like some sort of alien!" Hannah's shriek of laughter made Jackson look down at the cookie he was making. It *did* resemble an alien. He frowned and looked over at hers. Sure enough, she could make a perfectly shaped tree. He thought of something then, the memory of that night that now seemed so long ago.

"Hannah," he said, grabbing her by the waist, not caring that both their hands were filled with cookie dough as she willingly stepped into his arms. "I'm sorry about those damn cookies," he said gruffly, leaning down to capture her lips. She kissed him back easily and lovingly.

"You've been sampling cookies," he said between kisses. She pulled him closer, tugging at the back of his neck, and pretty soon Jackson was trying to decide whether or not she'd yell at him if he swept all her cookie dough off the counter and made love to her right then and there.

Jackson spotted her book bag by the kitchen table, reminding him that she still hadn't unpacked. Whenever she was done studying for the night, she'd pack up her books and stuff them into that Christmas bag. Even though he'd offered to share his home office space with her, she insisted it was more convenient for her to just store everything in her bag. She hadn't used her side of the closet for more than the wedding dress. She just kept a suitcase open on his luggage rack in the corner.

"Can I ask you something?"

"You're actually asking my permission?" she said with a

teasing smile.

"I try to be a gentleman," he said making a subtle attempt at snatching a cookie. She swatted his hand away.

"Why haven't you used any of the money I gave you?"

Her face went white then red.

"I haven't needed it." She shrugged, and then busied herself with plucking apart the gobs of dough he'd grouped together on the cookie pan.

"You haven't needed it?" He tried to be patient. She shook her head, tossing her hair over her shoulders, and he had to stifle a ripple of desire as the scent of her shampoo wafted over. "How did you pay for your tuition?"

She averted her eyes. "I charged it to one of my cards."

"It's ridiculous for you to go into debt when I've got more than enough to pay for your tuition."

She lifted her chin defiantly. "I'm not going into debt."

"Really? Then why would you charge your tuition to your credit card?"

"To get Air Miles, Jackson."

Air Miles. He took a deep breath. He needed to count to ten. "Planning on going somewhere?"

She shook her head, a smile tugging at her lips. "But I would bring you along if I were planning a trip."

"That's good to know," he said, moving a step closer to her. It was hard to stay mad at her. "But remember the deal we made. I'm paying your tuition."

"The deal I was forced into?"

"As I recall, Hannah, you were the one pounding down my door during a blizzard—"

"Only to have you slam it in my face."

The phone rang. It took them both a moment to register what the interruption was. Jackson leaned down to give her one more kiss, loving how disheveled she looked.

"Who is that?" Hannah asked, trying to straighten out her clothes as he glanced at the caller ID.

He put the phone back in his pocket. "Just work." He hated lying to her, but he'd have to call Nick back later. Guilt shot through him as Hannah stood there smiling and trusting.

"Want to go Christmas shopping?"

Hannah's eyes narrowed. "I'm sorry, I could have sworn that you just asked me to go Christmas shopping."

He snatched a cookie. "That's right. You, me, Em." He looked down at the cookie. "These are good. I don't think Ethan needs six of them. Two is more than enough. Give him the alien cookie I made."

"No, even Charlie wouldn't eat those," she said. Charlie lifted his scruffy head at the sound of his name, looked at the alien cookie, and shut his eyes again.

• • •

Jackson took a sip of the spicy, smooth Starbucks Holiday brew that Hannah had been relentlessly gushing about the last two weeks, while guiding Emily's stroller along the sidewalk.

"That's your new favorite coffee, isn't it? Admit it," Hannah said. He laughed, walking alongside her as they made their way home. "You're very pushy."

"Don't you *love* the Christmas design on the cup?"

Jackson held up his cup. Huh. Reindeer. "I never noticed before."

Hannah rolled her eyes. "It's the first thing I look for in November," she said, taking a swig.

"Please tell me you're joking." He smiled down at her, tempted to pull her in for a kiss, despite the crowds around them. But Hannah kept on going.

"And you secretly like Christmas shopping, don't you?"

This was probably one of the best days of his life. He looked from the gorgeous woman at his side, decked out in a red coat and jeans, holding her giant cup of coffee, to his niece contentedly sitting in the stroller. Fat, heavy snowflakes tumbled down as they walked along downtown Toronto. He gave Hannah a smile. "Fine, I like Christmas shopping. With you and Em," he said, slowing as they approached a streetlight.

"Oh, speaking of Christmas shopping, when do you want to deliver our gift to the Sampsons?"

Jackson groaned. "You didn't mention anything about us delivering the gift."

"Of course we're going to give it to them. Don't you think they'd love to see Emily again?" Hannah smiled up at him as they crossed the road.

Jackson spotted the man leaning against the corner of their building as soon as they stepped onto the sidewalk. The hairs on the back of his head rose instantly as their eyes made contact. Jackson slowed their pace, passing the stroller to Hannah.

"Jackson, what's wrong?" she asked, taking the stroller.

"I want you to go inside. I'll be up in a few minutes, okay?" He kept his eyes trained on the thin man with the disheveled hair, dirty jeans, and sweatshirt. He knew him. He *knew* that face. *Where?*

"What are you talking about?"

"Just trust me." His instincts were still sharp, fine-tuned to anything threatening. He needed to get Emily and Hannah inside. But before Hannah and Emily could get into the building, the man swaggered forward, a smirk on his unshaven face.

"Jackson Pierce?" he called out, his voice thick and confident.

"Who are you?"

"I'm that baby's father."

Chapter Fourteen

Jackson tried to ignore the sound of Hannah's gasp and concentrate on this low-life.

"Like hell you are. Go inside," he said, his eyes not leaving the man's face. He needed to remember where he'd seen him.

"No," he heard Hannah whisper frantically.

"Jackson Pierce, right? That's what you're calling yourself now?" The man smirked. Anger burst through him. This was the man claiming to be Emily's father? Jackson reigned in every single urge he had to sink his fist into the other man's face. Every fiber of his being wanted to hear that skinny jaw snap on impact. Revulsion slammed through him as he remembered this guy trashing his house, looking for money. This was not Emily's father.

"I remember you," Jackson said, keeping his voice steady.

"Glad to hear it. Too bad Louise is dead, she was a nice piece of—"

"I'd stop talking if I were you."

The man looked at Jackson and then gave Hannah a thorough once over. "But I gotta say this one is a definite step up."

Jackson bolted forward, pushing the man against the building, his forearm pinning him until Jackson felt him struggling under him to form words. His eye went to the small alleyway between the buildings. For a second he wished he was that adolescent that acted first and thought later.

He leaned down, letting his anger show, letting the carefully controlled emotions surface. "You stay the hell away from my family. You don't look at my wife. You don't talk to her. You don't talk about her."

"I came for the baby."

"She's not yours."

"I'm willing to negotiate. Your sister always said you were gonna be rich."

Jackson moved his face closer, disgusted by the stench of cheap liquor. "I came from nothing, just like you. I know how to fight dirty, and I swear to you I will. I will make you regret the day you ever thought about my daughter, or looked at my wife. I keep what's mine. Don't you forget that. So get your sorry ass away from my family." Jackson pinned him harder against the wall, not seeing the man anymore, only the threat.

"Jackson." Hannah's soft voice broke through his rage. He clenched his teeth and looked over at her, took in the pallor of her face, the trembling of her chin. And all the words she'd ever spoken to him about her childhood rang through his mind, all the violence she'd had to face. He glanced down at Emily—asleep, angelic, innocent. And then he stared at the lowlife in front of him, and Jackson thought of his and Louise's father, and he knew he couldn't do it. He couldn't raise his fists in anger in front of Hannah or Emily. Not ever.

"Stay the hell away from my family," Jackson said in a low voice, before releasing him and backing away.

The man clutched his throat, trying to take deep breaths and staring at Jackson with so much hatred that Jackson knew in his gut this wasn't over.

"Let's go," he said, turning to Hannah, forcing himself to calm down. He needed to be composed. He needed to be her rock. Jackson grabbed her hand and the stroller, ushering them toward the entrance. The doorman opened the doors for them and they were swallowed into the luxurious marble lobby. He turned around to look out the windows as they waited for the elevator. His eyes scanned the crowds of people, but the man was gone.

· · ·

Hannah didn't say a word. She couldn't look over at Jackson. She followed him into the apartment and just stood in the entryway, vaguely aware of Jackson taking Emily out of her stroller and walking out of the room. She stood there, coat still on, listening to the sounds she'd allowed herself to get accustomed to.

When Jackson returned, his face was haggard, his eyes filled with pain. "She didn't wake up," he said, his voice strained. He threw his keys and coat on the leather chair at the entry. Hannah couldn't bring herself to speak.

Jackson walked over to her. "I, uh, I'm sorry if I scared you."

Hannah shook her head, looking up at him. He hadn't scared her. He'd made her feel safe. He'd fought for her. In so many ways they came from the same place.

"He said he's her father."

Jackson nodded slowly, his lips narrowing.

Why had she let herself get her hopes up? Why did she think that things would be different this time? This was just like all the times she'd get pulled out of a good home. Someone would come to the door and tell them it was time for Hannah to leave. It was always too soon. In the good homes it was always too soon. And now it was happening to Emily. No one had loved Hannah enough to adopt her, but they loved Emily. That should be enough. This couldn't be happening. Hannah shook her head, she couldn't look at Jackson, couldn't wrap her arms around him, the shock of it all immobilizing her.

Her vision blurred as she felt Jackson's chest tuck against her, his strong arms encircling her. She felt his pain in the words that neither of them were capable of speaking. She didn't want to turn around to face him. She shivered back the sobs that threatened as he pressed his lips against her neck. This was it—she had failed. She couldn't save Emily. Their family was going to be ripped to shreds. They couldn't compete against her father.

"No one can take her away from us." She could hear the raw emotion in his voice as he whispered in her ear. She turned in his arms and looked up at him. His jaw was set, his dark eyes glittering. Hannah shook her head as his warm, strong hands cupped her face.

"You don't understand. Her father will win…you're just an uncle…there's a process. We will lose against her father."

"I'm swearing to you right now, no one is going to take Em away from us. I promise you—"

"You can't promise, no one can. I knew this would happen. I failed her," Hannah said clutching the fabric of his shirt.

"No you didn't," he whispered against her hair. "We haven't lost yet."

Hannah felt the kisses along her hair straight to her heart. After tonight, there would be no point in the two of them pretending to be married anymore. Her hands ran up the smooth cotton of his shirt, feeling the taught muscles clench. She tightened her hold on him. He cradled her face in his hands, kissing her with a wanting and yearning that she understood and matched kiss for kiss.

"Make it go away, Jackson, make the pain go away." He groaned and looked down at her, restrained desire etched in his face. He reached down to cup her bottom, lifting her so that she straddled him. She wrapped her legs around his waist, her mouth not leaving his. Wild and filled with a pain that was doubled because of his, they loved each other, clothes falling away, until there was nothing left between them.

Hannah reached up, tilting his head to within an inch of hers. "Now" she whispered, her words cut off as he captured her mouth in a frantic kiss and he entered her with barely restrained passion.

She felt the hard length of him. He filled her completely, filling the void, the loneliness. Until all that was left for her to do was surrender—surrender to the bliss that Jackson offered. And seconds after her world exploded, she felt him join her.

• • •

Jackson woke to the sound of coffee percolating and the smell of lemon cranberry muffins. He smiled faintly. In spite of everything that happened last night, the thought of Hannah still made him smile. She had spent much of the night pacing and holding Emily, and the one time when she'd been awake lying next to him, he'd made love to her slowly and sweetly until both of them forgot the pain and surrendered to the love that neither would admit out loud.

Hannah wasn't singing that song about the five ducks this morning. He hadn't realized how much he liked that song until now. He shrugged on a pair of jeans and walked barefoot towards the kitchen, thanking God for Hannah. They would get through this together, they would fight for Emily.

Jackson stopped cold. Her bags were piled neatly in the

hallway. The holly and berry bag was stuffed with books.

"Hannah?" he called out, walking into the kitchen. She stood with her back to him. When she slowly turned around he saw streaks down her face where she'd obviously been crying. She held up her hand and those glorious green eyes filled up with tears.

"I'm leaving."

"Why?" he felt anger and fear jog through him.

"Nicholas just called. How long have you known about Emily's father?"

• • •

Hannah tried to speak past the tears.

She had picked up the phone on the first ring when she'd seen it was their lawyer, and when Nicholas had mentioned his conversation about Emily's biological father with Jackson, she'd felt the burn of his betrayal.

Hannah wiped the tears away with trembling hands, hating standing here, like this, in the room that twenty-four hours ago had been filled with a babbling baby and a smiling Jackson. She stared at his tense face, hating how even now that he was the most gorgeous man she'd ever known.

He cringed. "I'm sorry, sweetheart. I didn't want you to panic—"

"You *lied* to me. How long have you known this?"

He looked away for a moment. "The night of our wedding."

Hannah put her hands over her face. This was a mess. He had lied. Emily's father was back. And she was…

"I was trying to protect you."

"Emily is going," she whispered, her voice shaking. He walked up to her and held her shoulders, the power in his hands reminding her of last night. The gentleness, the passion…

"No," he said slowly. "Stop thinking like we've lost. Paternity results aren't in."

Hannah shook her head, his words not registering. "If he's her father, he will gain custody. No matter how good Nicholas Wright is, we won't be able to adopt her."

"You know I will never let them take her. Think about this rationally. He's an addict, he's after money, not a baby. Emily is ours and we'll never lose her. I'm a fighter and so are you." He pulled her against him. She resisted for the briefest of seconds, not wanting to share her pain, not wanting to be comforted. But she couldn't resist the shelter he offered and she buried her face against his chest, crying for Emily, crying for them, crying for herself. Her kingdom of dreams belonged in her books, in her fantasies. He'd broken down her walls, and she'd been seduced by his kindness, his touch, his vulnerabilities. And now she was going to lose everything.

"I can't do it," she said against his chest, holding him tightly.

"I'll fight for both of us. You won't have to say goodbye to her," he said, his lips brushing her hair.

"You don't understand how much this would kill me. If you care about me you have to let me go," she whispered, still not moving away from him. She felt his body tense against her.

"Hannah," he said, as she finally gained the strength she needed to pull herself out of his arms, out of this false sense of security.

"Please, Jackson." She heard Emily begin to stir on the baby monitor and froze. She felt him watching her closely, and then Emily cried out again. She needed to go before he went to get Emily.

"Fine," he said roughly. "If this is what you need to do, then go. But I swear to God, I'm going make everything right. I'm not going to lose you or Em."

She didn't meet his eyes, just turned and walked down the hallway, pausing to pick up her two bags. She had to get out now. She felt her body tremble as she heard Emily begin to cry, and his voice call after her. "When you're ready, I'll be here."

She shut the door on his words, on Emily's cries.

Chapter Fifteen

Hannah took a deep breath, letting the cold December air fill her lungs as she stumbled out onto the bustling sidewalk. But she couldn't keep pace with the pedestrians, she couldn't move forward, she couldn't keep walking away from the only two people in the world that she truly loved. The Santa on the street corner jingled his bell and the image of Jackson in Hope's Crossing rushed through her mind. He'd fought for her, defended her, saved her. Jackson had taken the leap of faith. She had begged him to adopt Emily, to fight for his neice, and he had kept his promise. And now it was Hannah who was running the minute things got tough. She had spent so many years running. She understood why he had lied to her. He was the protector. He did it for his mother, his sister, and now for her and Emily. There was no way she could walk away from Jackson. She had to go back.

She slowly turned around when she heard her name above the noise of traffic and pedestrian chatter. It was the deep, rich voice that said her name like no one else could. There he was. Jackson stood tall and straight in the middle of the sidewalk, his black coat covered with snow.

Her eyes left his for a moment and her step faltered, as it had that night she'd found Emily. Jackson wasn't alone. In his arms, in complete contrast to his black coat, was a pink bundle. The world slowed for a moment, even as Jackson rushed toward her. Through the blur of tears, the haze of disbelief, she knew. Even though she had walked out on him, he was here for her.

"Hannah," he said roughly.

"Jackson."

He lifted his free hand to her cheek. He was real.

"I'm sorry I lied to you, and I know you said you needed time, but, hell, I can't let you go."

"I was on my way to you," she said, laughing and crying at the same time. "I'm sorry I walked out on you."

"I love you. You are the woman I want to spend the rest of my life loving every single day. I don't want a day to go by that I don't get to kiss you or hold you. You, Hannah. I want you forever." He stepped closer to her, wiping the tears that ran down her face. "I want you and Emily. Forever. If you'll have me, of course," he said with that smile that echoed his love.

She took a deep breath. "Emily?"

"I know that guy is a sham. You know it too. Emily is ours, but you need to believe it. And if we have to fight for her, we will. And we'll win," he said, brushing a kiss on Emily's forehead.

Jackson held Emily out to her. A love that she couldn't describe filled her heart and healed her soul as the baby stared, unblinking, at her, before breaking out into a wobbly grin. She couldn't walk away from this baby. She had fought so hard for her, lost a job for her, battled a blizzard for her. She couldn't give her up now. Not ever.

She looked up from Emily's angelic face to Jackson's. She

smiled up at him. "I love you too."

"I want us to find a home together—whatever you want. If you want to live in Hope's Crossing then we will. I want you to have a home of your dreams. We're going to be the family neither one of us never had. The real thing, Hannah. I want to be your husband. God, I want to be that man."

"Wherever you and Emily are is my home." When she felt his embrace and breathed in the scent of him, Hannah knew she was home. Jackson was home. Not a house, not a structure, him. She lifted her face to his, seeing love and the flickering of desire as he lowered his head to meet her mouth. She tasted forever on his lips as they stood in the snow, Emily nestled between them. She had found her knight, her kingdom of dreams.

Hannah had found her family for Christmas.

She had found her family forever.

Epilogue

"Daddy, don't forget the star!"

Jackson looked down at Emily who was staring up at him with wide brown eyes, clutching a sparkling gold star in her hand. He smiled as he leaned down and lifted his three-year-old daughter into his arms. The soft, red velvet fabric of her dress brushed against his forearm as he positioned Emily close to the tree top. He secured the ornament and chuckled as she clapped her hands at the finished product.

He walked over to the window facing the snow-covered front yard, still holding Emily in his arms. The sight outside was something he would never tire of—their front yard at the cabin was lit up like Vegas.

Hannah and Emily had spent all day adding white lights to the evergreens and wreaths and a Santa sleigh on the porch. Every year Hannah insisted that a giant wreath be hung on the front door. She had even managed to coerce him into climbing up a ladder and adding lights along the roof line. But he didn't complain. This year, he might even admit that he liked it.

"When's Auntie and Uncle Sampson coming, Daddy?" Emily asked, peering out the window. Jackson sighed. That was another annual tradition Hannah had started — the Sampsons on Christmas Eve. Another thing he didn't complain about. How could he when the elderly couple doted on his daughter as if they were her grandparents?

"Soon, sweetie. Just listen for bells," Jackson said, turning as he heard Hannah's footsteps.

His wife approached them, holding her index finger to her lips. "He's finally sleeping," Hannah whispered, snuggling up to his side.

"Baby Christopher sleeps too much!" Emily exclaimed with a frown.

"It just seems like that, Emily. But newborns need a lot more sleep that we do," Hannah said, tapping Emily's nose.

The exuberant jingling of bells indicated that the Sampsons were approaching. Jackson sighed and looked down at Hannah.

"I love you, Jackson," she said with a gorgeous smile and a sparkle in her green eyes as she pinched his side.

"Love you too, Hannah," he said, placing a kiss on her soft mouth. Kissing Hannah was something he never tired of. In fact, it was what he intended on spending a long time doing after the Sampsons left.

Emily laughed and bounced in his arms as the couple pulled into the driveway. A large red sack was stuffed into the rear of the sleigh.

"They're so sweet," Hannah whispered as she stared out the window.

Jackson agreed, but silently thought his wife was much sweeter. The woman by his side had shown him the power of forgiveness. They had a daughter in Emily, and two months ago, they welcomed a son. Jackson had learned the meaning of unconditional love.

And because of Hannah, he'd learned that holiday miracles did come true.

About the Author

Victoria James is a romance writer living near Toronto. She is a mother to two young children, one very disorderly feline, and wife to her very own hero. Victoria attended Queen's University and graduated with a degree in English Literature. She then earned a degree in Interior Design. After the birth of her first child she began pursuing her life-long passion of writing.

Her dream of being a published romance author was realized by Entangled in 2012. Victoria is living her dream-staying home with her children and conjuring up happy endings for her characters.

Victoria would love to hear from her readers! You can visit her at www.victoriajames.ca or Twitter @vicjames101 or send her an email at Victoria@victoriajames.ca.

Keep your Indulgence going with these
bestselling contemporary romances...

A Risk Worth Taking by **Victoria James**

When tragedy strikes, high-powered designer Holly
Carrington steps up to raise her orphaned niece. But to
secure the baby's future she must return to her hometown
and face the memories of all she has lost. Can small-town
bachelor Quinn convince Holly to give up her big-city
dreams and risk her heart, or will they set themselves up for
heartbreak...again?

The Best Man's Baby by **Victoria James**

Florist Claire Holbrook has *always* played by the rules her
entire life, but breaks them to spend one night with sexy
lone wolf Jake Manning. Six weeks later she discovers they
created a bond that will last a lifetime... Jake has *never*
played by the rules. Getting Minister Holbrook's daughter
pregnant wasn't part of any life plan, but he won't run from
his responsibilities. He'll step up and be the best man he
can, even if he doesn't have a clue where to begin.

Fair Play **by Tracy Ward**

Who knew writing three plays for a nationally acclaimed theater in Phair, Texas, would put Ashlyn Carter's inheritance at risk and force her into constant contact with the very guy she loves to hate? But Noah Blake is her muse and the spark of passion she'd felt for him as a teenager flares up again. Maybe Noah isn't the enemy the way she once thought.

Seven Night Stand by Nicole Helm

Reality TV scout Vivvy Marsh loves her job, but she'll lose it if she doesn't find a hit. When she's sent to Kansas to scout a show, it looks like a bust…until she meets sexy pilot, Nate Harrington. Nate can't deny his attraction to Vivvy, but no way can he let this show take off. The Harrington family is riddled with secrets, and she wants it all out in the open. For the next seven days, he's going to stop at nothing to keep her out of his family's business, even if it means keeping her distracted in his bedroom.

Endless Possibilities...
Check out these exciting titles from Entangled Embrace!

One taste is never enough...
SNEAKING CANDY
by Lisa Burstein

All I ever wanted was to make a name for myself as Candice Salinas, creative writing grad student at the University of Miami. Of course, secretly I already *have* made a name for myself: as Candy Sloane, self-published erotic romance writer. Though thrilled that my books are selling and I have actual *fans*, if anyone at UM found out, I could lose my scholarship...and the respect of my faculty advisor, grade-A-asshole Professor Dylan.

Enter James Walker, super-hot local barista and—*surprise!*—my student. Even though I know a relationship is totally off-limits, I can't stop myself from sneaking around with James, taking a few cues from my own erotic writing... if you catch my drift. Candy's showing her stripes for the first time in my real life, and I've never had so much fun. But when the sugar high fades, can my secrets stay under wraps?

There is no escaping fate…
FORGED BY FATE
by Reese Monroe

He's waited more than 900 years to love her…

Being the Gatekeeper to Hades is no small feat, and waiting almost a millennia to meet your mate is damn near impossible. But Theo Bradford's mark has finally surfaced on his intended. Now all he has to do is find her and convince her to embrace her supernatural heritage.

Young genius, Sadie Nowland, has got life figured out. Graduating college at the age of eighteen and accepting a six-figure job is just what she needs to prove she's made something of herself. But when a strange tattoo mysteriously appears on her shoulder and Theo starts talking about *Mates*, it catapults her neatly laid out life into chaos.

Targeted by a vicious demon escaped from Hades, Sadie is thrust into the volatile world of Shomrei warriors and a connection to Theo her brain can't comprehend and her body can't deny. That primal bond proves more imperative to their survival than either could have ever imagined—and just may be the key to the world's survival.

Hell is looking for a way to break loose…
RUINED
by Jus Accardo

Jax lost the genetic lottery. Descended from Cain, the world's first murderer, he's plagued by a curse that demands violence in exchange for his happiness. He left everything behind, including the girl he loved, but thriving on the pain of others is lonely… And it's killing him.

After a series of heartbreaking losses, Samantha put rubber to pavement and headed for college as fast as her clunker could carry her. But she can't outrun her problems. When an attack at school drives her back home, she's thrown into the path of a past—and a guy—she's been trying to forget.

Sam strains Jax's control over his darkness, but running isn't an option this time. Someone—or, *something*—followed her home from school: a ruthless monster with a twisted plan centuries in the making. Forced together to survive, and fighting an attraction that could destroy them both, Jax and Sam must stop a killer bent on revenge.

It's hard not to answer when trouble comes knocking…
TROUBLE COMES KNOCKING
by Mary Duncanson

A girl who can't forget…

Twenty-two-year-old Lucy Carver is like Sherlock Holmes in ballet flats, but her eidetic memory is more albatross than asset, and something she usually keeps hidden. When she notices that something's amiss at her dead-end job, she jumps at the chance to finally use her ability for good. That is, until a man is murdered, and she becomes the target of the killer.

A detective on his first case…

Detective Eli Reyes is overbearing, pompous, way too hot for Lucy's own good, and seems as determined to ruin her relationship with her boyfriend, John, as finding the murderer. He brings Lucy in on the case, thinking she can help him get to the truth, only to cut her loose when he realizes he's gotten far more than he ever bargained for.

A past that won't go away…

When memories from her childhood invade her present, Lucy discovers a mystery bigger than she could have imagined. With the killer still after her, and Eli nowhere to be found, she takes things into her own hands, determined to expose the truth no matter what—before trouble comes knocking… again.

Her theory of attraction is about to get a new angle...

DEFINITELY, MAYBE IN LOVE
by Ophelia London

Spring Honeycutt wants two things: to ace her sustainable living thesis and to save the environment. Both seem hopelessly unobtainable until her college professor suggests that with a new angle, her paper could be published. Spring swears she'll do whatever it takes to ensure that happens.

"Whatever it takes," however, means forming a partnership with the very hot, very privileged, very conceited Henry Knightly.

Henry is Spring's only hope at publication, but he's also the über-rich son of a land developer and cash-strapped Spring's polar opposite. Too bad she can't help being attracted to the way he pushes her buttons, both politically and physically. As they work on her thesis, Spring finds there's more to Henry than his old money and argyle sweaters...but can she drop the loud-and-proud act to let him in? Suddenly, choosing between what she wants and what she needs puts Spring at odds with everything she believes in *Definitely, Maybe in Love* is a modern take on *Pride and Prejudice* that proves true love is worth risking a little pride.

He's loved her. Killed for her. Yet he may not be able to save her.

HUSHED
by Kelley York

Eighteen-year-old Archer couldn't protect his best friend, Vivian, from what happened when they were kids. Since then, he's never stopped trying to shelter her from everything else. It doesn't matter that Vivian only uses him when skipping from one toxic relationship to another. Archer is always there, reeled in and tossed out, waiting to be noticed.

Then Evan Bishop breezes into town with a warm smile and calming touch, and Archer can't deny his attraction to him. Evan is the only person who keeps him around without a single string attached. And the harder Archer falls for Evan, the more he sees Vivian for the manipulative hot-mess she really is.

But Viv has her hooks in deep, and once she finds out Archer's dark secret, she threatens to expose the truth if she doesn't get what she wants. And what she wants is for him to end his relationship with Evan...permanently.

CPSIA information can be obtained
at www.ICGtesting.com
Printed in the USA
LVHW091413030820
662249LV00002B/636

9 781503 056145